OXFORD HEAT

Hannah Haze

Want to read another Hannah Haze omegaverse for free?

Visit Hannah's website
www.hannahhaze.com

CHAPTER ONE

Oxford, Christmas 2016

She's risking it. Sitting here alone in the library is dangerous.

Her skin boils and her muscles ache. The gland at the back of her neck tingles and her gut cramps.

She should leave. Her heat is starting. She shouldn't be out in public like this.

Instead, she strips off her coat, her jumper and her top, and sits in her vest and jeans, scratching at her gland. The ancient heating groans through the pipes, barely warming the vast space, the temperature cool, and yet she feels so hot.

Only one light shines in the dark library, illuminating her desk, and the windows glimmer around her like inky paintings. The balcony that runs the circumference of the cylindrical building is empty, the shelves of books wrapped in blackness, and the reading tables bare.

Outside, the college buildings stand deserted. Strings of lights streak over the buildings, but nobody there to see them. The university faculties, the Oxford union, and the various cafeterias are all shut up too. Only this library, the Bodleian, remains open for students.

Tonight, with Christmas only days away, she is alone, and so she's made herself comfortable, dragging all the cushions over to a corner and spreading out her books and an array of snacks. She's forbidden to eat in the library, but the librarians left for the holidays two days ago and she's seen nobody else here for the past twenty-four hours.

Her phone rests on a bookcase. Earlier she blasted out some hard rock because she's bored to death of cheesy Christmas songs and dreary love ballads. Now she's opted for the tick of some unseen clock and the swish of distant cars. She yawns and rubs her brow, scribbling down a note in her book.

Heats are something she doesn't enjoy. Painful, overwhelming and humiliating. She's on suppressants which allows her to have fewer than she would naturally and to time them for when she wants, so she times them for the holidays when she knows the flat she shares with her friend Rose will be empty and she can keep hidden away, not forced to miss classes, not drawing attention to herself.

She refuses to let herself be determined by her designation. She won't let her biology rule her present or dictate her future, and she will certainly challenge any preconceived ideas people have about her just because she's an Omega.

So what if she smells like sex? What does it matter if her gland throbs and dampness already pools between her legs? It's nobody else's business. And she's alone.

Except she isn't.

Her ears prick up at the sound of the heavy library doors opening on the far side of the building and then feet padding through. She shifts in her seat, her senses primped. An unease stirs in her belly but she sweeps it away as she pushes strands of hair from her face, and ducks her head closer to the page, staring at the words. A handle squeals, a lamp blinks on, and her pulse quickens. The flesh on her arms goose bumps and she grips her pen tight between her forefinger and thumb.

Then her nose catches it: *Alpha.*

The fierce, overpowering scent hits her right at the back of the head; a bullet to the brain.

This is dangerous. If an Alpha finds her here in heat...

She sits bolt upright, every hair on her skin prickling, her body frozen. If she remains still, he won't find her. But he'll smell her. Of course he will. Best to get out of here. She grabs her bag and rams her jumper and top inside. Then she glances at the rest of her stuff, not knowing where to start.

The scent is familiar, very familiar, thick and pungent in the air. It stands out, something about it different — like rich spice in a room of flowers. But her brain is in too much of a frenzy to identify it.

She yells inside her head, trying to force herself to move.

It works.

She stuffs her notebook, her pen and her laptop into her rucksack and picks up her phone from the shelf, slinging on her coat. The books and the snacks can be abandoned.

The smell of the Alpha is already doing funny things to her, making her insides go sloppy, her skin warm and her nipples hard. *Shit.* She needs to move her arse. She closes her eyes, attempting to calm herself, to pluck up the courage to move. The rows of books, an intermingling mish-mash of colours and sizes on the shelf, swim and swoop before her eyes. She forces herself to walk.

The shrill voice in her head screams. *Come on, pick up your feet, Cora. Not too fast. Don't run. Walk. Calm but quick. Eyes on the ground. Slip out the door.*

She can sense him near, the lights to her left flicking on, and there's the squeak of rubber soles on varnished floorboards. He is over there somewhere, his scent intensifying, and more lights dancing across the high library ceiling, following her movements as she weaves through the desks and in and out of the bookshelves.

She can't see him, but she can almost hear his heavy breath and her heart thumps so hard in her chest it hurts. She grips the strap of her bag until her fingernails sink into her palms, and her eyes lock on the exit, the heavy double doors drawing closer with every hurried step.

Then she's at the door, her trembling hand reaching for the handle.

Don't look back. Don't look back.

But she can't help it. Can't resist it. The urge is too strong.

So she turns her head, her eyes sweeping the rows. And there he is, Noah Wood.

Leaning against a wall, his dark hair hanging in his face and his body bathed in shadow.

She can't see his eyes but she knows he is watching her, every fibre in his body taut and alert. Like a sprinter poised for the starter's gun.

She swallows, unable to move. She shouldn't have looked. It is all the invitation he needs, and now she is screwed.

Because Noah is trouble. With a capital T. Underlined and bolded.

Turning around, she snatches open the door and hurries out, skipping down the library steps and along the cobbled road shimmering with the reflections of dull orange street lamps. The Christmas lights are all extinguished and the tall college buildings tower above her, blocking out the sky. She dashes through the puddles, able to smell him behind her even through the December drizzle.

Her coat pulled tight, snuggling her chin into her collar and clutching her bag, she reaches the silent roads, her home only three streets away. She tugs out her keys, ready to open the front door quickly, straining to catch his footsteps, but hearing only the hum of distant traffic.

He is there, though. She knows it. Her body confirming it in the way her blood thrums through her veins and her core aches, the cramps in her pelvis almost hampering her steady pace.

She could try to shake him off or head some place where there'd be other people. She could. She won't.

He is following. He is chasing. He wants her. She never thought someone like Noah Wood would want someone like her. Plain. Scrawny. Poor.

A pathetic example of an Omega. Taller than she should be, with slim hips and small tits, and an attitude to boot. Not your average submitting, placid, curvy little Omega.

Yet here he is. Hovering right behind her on the doorstep. Not touching her, not pressing her, not forcing her. Waiting.

With fumbling fingers, she snaps open the locks and steps inside the dim hallway, leaving the door open behind her. As she slips out of her coat and pulls off her boots, she hears him stride inside. When she turns, he is framed by the doorway. A hulk lurking in the darkness. Twice her size. Solid and strong. His eyes black like a moonless sky, his nostrils flared, his shoulders rising and falling with his heaving breaths.

"Shut the door," she says, trying to sound confident, firm, but her voice struggling from her lips in a timid whisper.

It's only the second time she's ever spoken to him.

The last time was a year ago.

A year ago

Cora sprints through the darkened Oxford streets, her feet rattling on the cobbled pavements, and her breath illuminated white swirls when she dashes beneath lampposts. As she flies around a corner, the scarf she's thrown around her neck flutters to the ground, and she curses, scooping down to pick it up and stuff it under her arm, already struggling to carry her rucksack and her notes.

When she reaches the town centre she finds it deserted, the doorways of the shops darkened except for the odd flicker of Christmas lights and the bright neon stars hung in neat rows along the high street. In the distance, the Old Union building stands lit up like a Christmas tree; the long windows glowing yellow against the cold winter's sky. As she draws closer, the building seems to hum from within and she can already smell the mixture of a hundred scents.

She knew it would be busy — tickets for tonight's speaker snapped up in a matter of minutes — but it is still a surprise to see the usually empty rack jostling with bikes, all chained together in forced angles.

Quickly, she dashes up the steps to the entrance, pushing against the heavy wooden doors.

"Evenin' Cora," says an elderly man who emerges from behind a small kiosk to the left of the door as she enters.

"Have they started?" she asks, panting, trying to untangle herself from her scarf and almost tripping as she does.

The old man smiles, and retrieves one end of the scarf, helping to free her.

"I think you've made it on time — sounds like they're still chatting in there."

"Thanks Ted," she pats his shoulder and trots down the corridor.

He is right, she can hear voices and when she pushes open the next door, she's hit by a wall of noise; the chamber as tightly packed as the bike rack, every wooden bench full as well as the balcony that runs around the dark red walls and people stood against the panelling at the back and to the sides.

She pushes her way through the people, finally making her way to one of the front rows and sliding into a remaining space.

"Cora," a small woman, with long dark hair, her roommate Rose, threads her arm through Cora's once she's shrugged off her duffel coat and removed her beret. "I didn't think you were going to make it."

"It was so busy in the cafe today — all the Christmas shoppers wanting a coffee on their way home — I didn't feel like I could just leave them."

Cora leans into her friend, resting her head against her shoulder. "You're not mad, are you?"

"No, of course not. I'm just sad you missed out on the pre-reception with Rosamund. I know she's your idol."

Cora squeezes Rose's hand. "I'm so excited to hear her speak! And I'm sure there'll be an opportunity afterwards to meet her." Cora lifts her head and peers behind her. "Who's here tonight?"

"Everyone!" Rose says.

"I can see nearly every Omega I know."

"That's hardly surprising. She's like the poster woman for the modern Omega. Independent, successful, outspoken."

"I want to be just like her when I grow up!"

"Did you spot all the Alphas at the back?" Rose asks, nudging her head in their direction.

Cora groans. "I'm surprised they came. They don't usually give a flying shit what an Omega has to say!"

Rose frowns with disapproval. "They are probably here to try to pick up Omegas."

"Probably," Cora says, although the interweaving scents of the Alphas and Omegas she can smell in the hall don't read that way. There is anticipation and excitement, so clear it is almost palatable on the air.

"I might just run down the hall and get something to eat from the vending machine." she says clutching her stomach as it growls with hunger. "I don't want everyone hearing my stomach all evening."

"Be quick or you'll miss it."

Cora grabs her purse and hurries to her feet. "Want anything?"

"Nope," Rose says, already back to scanning the audience.

Cora pushes her way through the crowd with mutters of "sorry" and finally makes it out of the hall and into the corridor. She trots quickly, trying to remember down which corridor the snack machine is located.

And then she stops in her tracks, nearly tumbling over her own feet.

Noah Wood.

She can't see him, but she can smell him, his scent overpowering, and when she starts walking again, and turns the corner, she can see why.

His towering frame blocks the width of the corridor, as he bounces an oval shaped ball on the dark polished floor. He's dressed in his rugby kit, his dark hair damp with sweat around his brow and his boots caked with mud.

Obviously, he's come straight from a match or practice — an up-and-coming star of the university team. And doesn't he know it? Not giving a shit about the mess he is making or the damage to the ancient university floors.

It's not surprising. He doesn't give a shit about anything or anyone. Only a few weeks ago he got into a fight in a bar in town and put the other guy in hospital. He should've been thrown out of the university; anybody else would have been. The only reason he didn't end up with charges pressed and an expulsion is probably his family. They say they are very wealthy and very influential. Money lets you get away with all sorts. It's why he never turns up to class but always gets top grades. She's certain he's paying someone to write his essays.

He doesn't look her way, not until she stops right beside him, and glares up into his caramel eyes, waiting for him to let her pass.

Then his eyes flick to hers, but he doesn't acknowledge her, and he doesn't step aside.

She takes a deep breath, determined not to be intimidated.

"Can I get by please?" she asks, raising her chin defiantly.

His head turns towards her, and his eyes are a little confused, as if he's been snatched from his thoughts. For a moment she wonders if perhaps he really hadn't known she was there, but then he continues to bounce his ball down onto the wooden floor, the boards thwacking each time, and gestures in front of him.

Sure, she could squeeze past, but why should she? Why can't he be polite for once and take a step back?

"You're making a mess!" she hisses in annoyance and he smirks. She folds her arms. "Why are you even here?"

He examines the motion of the ball. "Why shouldn't I be here?"

Because everyone knows he has no respect for Omegas. It's the other rumour associated with his name — that he passed on some photos of a girl he was seeing. People will pay an awful lot of money for that type of porn.

She tosses her head. "What, lurking about in the corridor, rather than actually coming to listen to what a prominent Omega has to say?!"

She thinks he almost flinches at that and lifts his gaze to meet hers. God, she can't stand him, but his eyes when he looks at her are always so intense, and she freezes to the spot, like prey trapped by the eyes of its predator. She knows it is probably an Omega reaction, but she hates it, hates being cornered.

Although, right now, she wonders if it is that or if it is the colour. His eyes are so unusual, beautiful even, a dark earthy brown in the centres that melt to gold around their rims. They are the sort of soft eyes fringed with long lashes that don't belong to a ruthless hunter.

The temperature of her skin creeps upwards and his eyes swim over her face. She doesn't move, her own eyes dropping slightly and landing on his lips. They are parted and she can make out the red of his tongue in his mouth.

Then his mouth opens and he swallows. "I'm waiting for my mum."

Her eyes flick back to his and a door behind her opens. He lifts his head, peering over hers.

"Noah!" a voice calls, and he tucks the white

ball under his arm and squeezes around her, trying to make every effort he can not to touch her. Cora turns as he passes and watches as he stalks towards the older woman dressed in a cream trouser suit who's called him, her hair smartly clipped in a blunt bob.

Cora's heart sinks to her toes, disappointment weighing down her shoulders.

Rosamund Wood.

Noah's mum is Rosamund Wood.

How could someone like her have a son like that?

Cora stares at the floor, clumps of mud and grass scattered over the wooden boards. She doesn't bother going to listen to the talk after that.

CHAPTER TWO

Oxford, Christmas 2016

Noah kicks at the door with his foot, his eyes fixed on her, and it shuts with a slam, making her jump like a frightened rabbit.

"Give me your phone," she says.

The skin below his eye twitches. "Why?" His voice is thick.

"You know why!" she spits and his nostrils flare, a look of disgust flying over his face, one that has the Omega inside her almost relenting. He glares at her, then tugs it from his pocket and flings it at her.

Yes, he knows why she won't trust him with a phone.

She grips it in her hand and stares back at him, his gaze heating her blood; the air between them mixed with their scents, both alert, both cautious, both aroused as hell. The strength of it is undeniable. He licks his lips, his gaze travelling down her body, hovering at the peaks of her nipples visible through the cotton of her vest, lingering at the fly of her jeans.

"You done this before?" he barks, his eyes still locked on her groin.

"No. Not like this." She's slept with other men. But it hadn't been like this. They hadn't smelt like this. They hadn't made her feel like this; weak at the knees and needy.

"But you want to?" he asks, one eyebrow creeping up his brow.

"Yes," she says, surprised by her certainty, her determination.

A spike of pain sears through her gut, and she clutches for the wall, slick sliding into the crotch of her knickers, filling the air with her tangy scent.

"Alpha!" she moans and he is on her, his hands gripping her arse, lifting her off her feet, his wet mouth on her neck; his tongue and his teeth grazing at her gland.

Nobody's touched her there before — her mating gland. Nobody's violated her like that. It's not somewhere you touch without permission. Trust Noah to break the rules. Trust her not to care. He doesn't pierce skin — it's not a claiming bite, one which would bind them together for life. He skirts around the edges of the boundaries, like he always does.

"Where's the bedroom?" he growls into her neck but they don't make it that far, because instead he presses her against the wall, ripping at her jeans and her underwear, and forcing them down her thighs, tugging himself free and plunging inside. He is big and the stretch has her sucking in breath through her teeth as he pushes further and further, gorging her.

As soon as he bottoms out, he pounds , not pausing for breath, keen, it seems, to pump her full of his seed as soon as possible. She wraps her legs around him, digging her nails into his shoulder, hissing in his ear like a snake, hating that he feels this good, cursing that it is him, wishing her body didn't love every moment, her back crashing into the wall with every violent thrust, his hands like vice, his body giving her everything it has.

She is so wet, so ready, so primed, that she dips easily over the edge, her frame shaking as her cunt quivers, and her orgasm crashes through her; the waves of pleasure sweeping away all thought.

He leans back to watch, his own release hitting, warm liquid flooding inside her as his tight jaw relaxes and his eyes soften.

"Omega," he whispers, grinding into her with every fresh shot and resting his damp forehead on her shoulder as he pants to catch breath.

Then he walks them through to her bedroom, lying them both carefully on the bed, unmade from the morning; dirty washing and mugs scattered about the place and the curtains still drawn.

That's when it hits.

Fuck! What has she done?

This is why there'd been so many lectures during Omega sex education lessons, drilling home the need to plan a heat ahead, for Omegas to make their decisions while they still have their senses.

Once in the throes of a heat, Omega's emotions and sexual desires take over, and Omega and Alpha sex isn't an average hook-up. An Omega can't grab their stuff and make a run for it if things don't work out, because the guy turns out to be an idiot or the sex crap.

No, he's in rut now, hard and coming again and again, which, if an Omega happens to be fucking their mate-for-life is pretty romantic, but if it is the man they loath, if the man is Noah fucking Wood, it is excruciating and embarrassing. And judging by his hardness, he'll be here fucking her for some time.

He stretches out, one arm flopping possessively over her waist; his eyes, back to their caramel brown now his pupils have shrunk, peering at her.

At least there are two advantages of being trapped here. Noah has always smelled mouth-watering, up close he smells even better, up close and in the middle of a rut he smells so good she doesn't possess the words to describe it. And he looks as good as he smells. Beautiful. His pale skin contrasting to his thick black hair, his lips full and red. A masculine Snow White.

But what does all that matter? His scent and his good looks are tainted. A dangerous taint that could infect her too. As delicious as he looks and smells, lying here with him makes her sick to the stomach.

The first time she laid eyes on him was in the lecture hall. The lecturer had asked for opinions and she'd given hers readily, happy to be somewhere where people cared about her thoughts and ideas. Then the lecturer had pointed to some boy at the back of the hall. She'd swivelled around in her seat to spot him. Tall and dark, so clearly an Alpha, sprawled out on his chair like he didn't give a shit. It was hard to miss him, huge and dominant, his scent seeming to fill even the huge cavernous space of the lecture hall.

After a pause, he'd tossed out some snarky comment and the other guys around him had sniggered, sneering down at her like she was a piece of meat, and the professor had frowned and quickly moved on. But she'd stayed glaring at him until his smiling gaze left his friends and swept across the hall, finally finding hers. His smile had melted into something else and it was in that moment she knew she hated him.

Luckily, he stopped going to lectures ages ago, and when she bumps into him outside class, he avoids her completely, refusing to meet her eye, his scent strong with something she wonders is disgust.

Because she's not like him — privileged and wealthy. And it seems to bother Noah Wood a lot.

How could she let this happen? And now she'll be forced to endure a trip to the sexual health clinic.

Happy Christmas, Cora!

At least she's on birth control, not that that is entirely foolproof when an Omega and Alpha are sharing a heat. She'll need to take a pregnancy test as well as one for STDs.

His face is still. He doesn't seem troubled by trivial things such as thoughts. She doubts Noah ever worries. What would someone with the odds stacked so overwhelming in their favour have to worry them?

He drags his tongue along his lip and she wonders if he is bored now the sex is over.

"Why are you still here at uni? Why haven't you gone home for Christmas?" he asks.

"I could ask you the same thing."

He sighs and then blows at the strands of hair that have fallen into his face. "My parents have buggered off on some tour around America. I didn't want to go."

"Why not?"

"I've been on enough of those types of trips already. They're fucking dull — being dragged from one place to another with nothing to do."

"Hmmm." She isn't convinced; dragged around America, rubbing shoulders with influential people, seeing amazing places, sounds the opposite of dull. "You haven't got brothers, sisters, friends to go see?"

"I have a brother. He's in the States too. He lives there." A shadow passes over his features.

"There's only two of you?" Most Alphas and Omegas she knows come from big families. Being an only child like herself is a rarity.

"Yes, just the two of us." He shifts on the bed.

"I'm going to my grandparents. But my grandad is a miserable old git who will spend the entire time lecturing me. I'm not going until I have to." He rubs his thumb over the ridge of her hip bone. Back and forth, gently. "How about you?"

"This is my home so...." She shrugs, and he cocks his head. "I'm too old for foster parents now."

His thumb halts and his eyes search her face. It feels invasive and she averts her own eyes, watching instead the rhythmic expansion of his rib cage.

"And your friends didn't invite you home for Christmas?"

"Well, Rose's flown back to Chicago, and there's no way I could afford the airfare."

He nods. "And the others?"

"Zach's Muslim. He doesn't celebrate Christmas." She shrugs again. "And anyway, I'm not bothered. Christmas is—" She pulls a face.

He laughs. "Yeah, it is."

She doesn't think he believes that. How could you when you have a family to spend it with?

"But why were you at the library alone like that, Omega?" he asks, searching her face a second time as if she is an unusually tricky puzzle he is debating how to solve. "It was fucking dangerous."

Wow, what a surprise, victim blaming.

"Why? Because I might bump into some deranged Alpha?" she jerks her chin at him, "like you."

"Are you complaining? You didn't seem to care about me being here five minutes ago when I was making you come."

"Ha!" She snorts.

"You liked it," he growls, gripping her waist.

She swallows. There's no point denying it. He would spot the lie in her eyes.

"Why did you follow an Omega on her own, then?"

"You wanted me to, I could read it in your scent."

She drops her gaze from his, her cheeks warming with the truth of it. "You chased me!"

"You let me in."

She scowls at him. "And now I need to get tested. Thanks for that."

His shoulders tense. "Fuck, aren't you on birth control?"

"Shouldn't you have asked me that earlier?" She shakes her head. "Of course I am."

"And I don't have any STDs," he snaps.

"Yeah, sorry if I don't take your word for it."

"Hmmm, in that case, perhaps I better get tested too then."

"I don't have anything."

He smirks at her, one eyebrow raised as if he's won a point from her in some game. "And how—"

"I haven't been with anyone since I broke up with my boyfriend six months ago and I got tested straight after."

His eyes widen. "But you must have—"

"Had a heat since then? Yes, but I had them alone."

"Why the fuck would you do that? A heat on

your own would be—"

"Miserable. But better than being with some arsehole Alpha."

His lips curl. "And how's that plan working out for you?"

She frowns, a deep crease forming between her eyebrows, her eyes narrowing. She doesn't like to lose an argument, not with someone like him. His cock is still buried inside her so she contracts her pelvic floor, squeezing him tightly, thinking she'll cause him some pain but finding the opposite.

"Ahhh," he groans, tipping his chin and closing his eyes. "Fuck, you feel so good."

Yes, she likes that too. Enjoys having him at her mercy. She squeezes him a second time, his hardness rubbing along her walls, knocking over a point that makes her gasp. She does it repeatedly, her eyes drifting shut as the head of his cock knocks into the spot and blots out all else.

"You want more?" he says and her eyes spring open at his voice. "You want more of me?"

"You know I do," she stutters.

He rolls her onto her back, clamping her hands above her head and trailing his gaze over her face, forcing her to wait. Then he climbs above her, thrusting himself downwards, and her eyelids flutter shut again as she dissolves into the sensation.

When she opens her eyes to peer up at him, there's another grin spreading across his face. She grinds her teeth and clenches, quick fire pulses designed to stir him up, and he grips her and rolls his hips, slowly, tantalising. She's going to make him suffer, to take him right to the edge of his orgasm and then leave him there suspended. But she doesn't have the control, her body succumbs to his, his pace winding up, his drives powerful, his hands sliding underneath her to grasp at her backside and bury himself ever deeper. The smug look on his face morphs to concentration, his brow furrowing and his hair dampening with his sweat.

If the first time was a quick, hard fuck — this is something different altogether. This time he seems to want to make it last, to draw it out, to watch as he stirs her up, the tension in her cunt and in her pelvis building gradually and gradually, strengthening and strengthening until her whole body is tight as an elastic band, and the pressure rings in her ears. Her teeth grip together, her fingers struggle for purchase in the sheets, and her vision swims with tears.

And then she releases. Like water bursting through a dam, her body falls lax, her spine arches and pure bliss pours outwards from her core to the tips of her fingers and the ends of her toes.

He doesn't let up. He wants to make her come again, his thumb finding its way to work at her clit, triggering another orgasm and then another, until finally he comes too, filling her belly with spunk, then collapsing heavily onto her chest, sweaty and boneless. He lies there panting for several minutes and the crush of him is both immense and welcome and her nerves seem to sing with the afterglow of her climax, her reality both heightened and dreamlike.

He inhales deeply, once, twice, catching his breath and then he stirs, sweeping her damp hair from her neck, kissing her there and wrapping his arms securely around her as if he's determined not to let her go.

"You're an angry little Omega," he chuckles as she drifts into sleep, the tiredness of her body overtaking her mind.

Much later in the night she wakes to find her mouth parched dry and her stomach cramping. He is still there, lying sprawled out on his stomach, his limbs spread wide like he owns the bed. Of course, he won't leave now until her heat is over. Why would he?

His scent hangs in the room too, thick and heavy, stamping his mark on her and her nest. She huffs and clambers to her feet, her legs shaky and her body boiling hot. Stripping off her vest, she hobbles to the kitchen, come streaming down her thighs. The sink is stacked full of dirty dishes, without Rose to nag her she hasn't bothered to wash up, and there is a growing line of empty wine bottles. Standing on her tiptoes, she reaches up for a glass and runs the water until it is ice cold, then gulps down several mouthfuls, aware of him moving in the bedroom and stalking down the hallway. This time, there's no request for permission. He twines his arms around her belly and nuzzles into her neck.

"I would have got that for you."

"I'm perfectly capable of getting myself a glass of water."

"Yeah, but I don't want you leaving that bed." His hard cock nudges against the cheeks of her backside. "Hmmm you taste amazing," he says, his tongue finding her gland.

She leans her head forward, away from his mouth. "Don't do that."

"You liked it earlier," he whispers, chasing her neck, clamping his mouth on her gland, sucking so hard her knees buckle. "You like it now too, don't you?"

"Yes," she stutters, dropping her glass in the sink and gripping the countertop.

"Back to bed, Omega." He slaps her arse and moves aside, waiting for her to pass by.

She staggers, and he scoops her up as if she weighs nothing at all, carrying her back down the hallway.

The pain in her stomach flares and she scrunches up her eyes. "Make it stop," she whispers.

He stares down at her, halting at the edge of the bed and flinging her across the mattress, her legs trailing over the edge. "I'm going to take care of you, Omega, until this is over. Anything you need,

I'm going to give you. And right now you need me."

She wants to make some snarky reply, but it will only delay him, and what she wants more, like he said, is him inside her, her slick already leaking into the sheet. He looks magnificent towering over her. There is no other word that gives him justice. His body is all tightly packed muscle, the ridges pulling taut against his skin, a strength radiating from him, a power that makes her feel tiny and weak in comparison. He could crush her if he chose to. Instead, he offers up his body, using his strength to pleasure her. She wonders if this is what it is like to be worshipped.

Clasping her hips, and angling her arse upwards so he can line himself up, he plunges in, hitting the spot that has her pain exploding into pleasure.

The frame of the bed shakes violently with every thrust, his fingers creeping around to discover her clit as he sends her into a frenzy of frustration. She needs her release desperately, chasing her orgasm with clenched teeth and tensed shoulders, fisting at the sheets, but not wanting him to play her so easily, wishing her body would understand this man is bad news.

But it's futile. His body seems designed to fit hers, to hit all the right places, to perceive just what she needs and how. The ecstasy smashing through her blows away her thoughts and her reservations.

"Harder," she moans, surprising herself by how much she longs to be pulverised, surrendering to him, no longer holding back, opening her legs as wide as she can and allowing him to fuck her completely.

When he's finished, they don't speak, and he rolls them onto their sides, his hand trailing up and down the curves of her hip, the scoop of her waist and the swell of her breast. His touch is faint, and the sensation lulls her back into sleep.

Later she wakes, and the sky is light with the dull December day, the patter of rain audible at the window, and, to her surprise, a collection of snacks are piled on the nightstand along with a jug of water. The pain and the need rumble in her gut and she moans. Noah stirs, seeming to sense she's awake and needing him. He says nothing, just drags her back against his body, gliding his hardness along the cheeks of her arse until he finds her entrance and slides inside.

What is this? The seventh, eighth time? She'd lost count as the night had morphed into day and then back to night, the memory of it a mix of heat and fever, fucking and coming, pleasure and pain. The bed is a mess of soiled sheets, pulled from the mattress, hanging off the frame, and the room stinks of what they've done.

He's had her over and over, and yet even now as he drives his way into her, she's still taken aback by the sensation. How big he feels, how far he stretches her open, making room for himself, reaching deeper within her than anyone ever has. It whips her breath away every time, and though she hates him, hates him with every passing moment they are together, she knows she would happily, gratefully, do this with him again and again. Just for this alone.

Like her, he's clearly exhausted, and he fucks her sleepily this time, as he laps at her neck, his hands cupping her breasts, squeezing them and rolling her hardened nipples between his fingers. She closes her eyes and drifts away, the orgasm rocking through her dreamily until she hardly knows if she is awake or not.

Hours must have passed when she wakes with a start the final time. Her heat is withering but the need still aches in her belly and it makes her irritable so she can't help snapping at him when she finds him sitting alongside her, flicking through one of her notebooks.

"Hey!" she says, lunging at the book. He snatches it out of her reach. "That's mine, and it's private." She can't quite remember what she has in that notebook, probably a few doodles, the odd sketch, and maybe an observation or a poem. But it is private, somewhere she captures her ideas, and she doesn't want him rifling through them.

"You took my phone away. What else do you expect me to do?"

She points to the rows of textbooks on the shelf on the opposite wall. "Read one of those."

He snorts and flings the book back at her. "Why have you always gotta be such a grumpy bitch?"

Tugging the sheet, she snarls. He means opinionated. He means assertive. Men don't like that, especially the Alphas. In fact, most *people* don't like it. Foster parents, social workers, school teachers. They only want you to express your views in the boxed places and times they decide. They trumpet their phrases — 'never be afraid to say how you feel' or 'you can always talk to me' — but they don't mean it. She's learnt that. It is better to keep your feelings buried inside. And she tries so hard to do that, but sometimes they come leaking out. "Because I don't like you."

He flinches, ever so slightly, but she catches sight of it. "You don't know me."

"Oh, but I do." She pulls herself up to kneeling. "I know your *type* alright."

"Right." His jaw tightens. "And what is my type?"

"The type who doesn't give a shit about anyone else — only yourself." There were plenty of those at school, at some of the estates she'd lived in, even among the people employed to look out for her. Some would pretend otherwise. Noah doesn't even care enough for that.

"And you think you do care about other people?" He chuckles. "Because you go on your little marches and write your earnest articles in the student paper. You think you're some social justice warrior. You're not; you're pretentious."

"It's not pretentious to care about people — to want to make the world a better place." What else could you do? All the wrongs and the evils and the frustrations. Everything operates ineffectively — she can see the wheels in the mechanics — where things are poorly built, where they don't fit together, or where they stall or catch. She wants to fix it — her fingers itching with the need to do it.

"It's all just hot air! Virtue signalling." He shakes his head.

It's not. There's plenty she does, that she tries to do. Talks at her old secondary school, trying to motivate the students to work hard and apply to a university like hers, mentoring two first years from disadvantaged backgrounds. She's even got a shift booked at the soup kitchen once this heat is over. However, those aren't things she talks about, they're private, and he'd sneer at them like he sneers at everything people like her try to do to make a difference.

She glares at him. "The world seems good to you because you're an Alpha and a privileged one at that."

"Like I said, you don't know me."

"I've seen enough of you to take the measure of you." She dips her head at him. "Trust me."

His brow darkens and anger flashes in his eyes. "Then why the hell am I here?"

She doesn't have an answer for that. She doesn't know.

"Time for me to go then." He springs from the

bed and stomps about the room, gathering up his clothes. "Your heat is pretty much over, anyway."

It isn't. She can sense there is at least another half day of it to go, and he knows that too.

But maybe it is for the best, even if her skin pricks and her stomach cramps as she watches him pull his t-shirt over his sculpted torso, and boxers up over his thick thighs, tucking his erection inside. He observes her from the corner of his eye as he dresses, neither of them speaking.

She doesn't want him to go, and yet she can't wait for him to leave. Her body and her mind battling inside, adding to the exhaustion and confusion from her heat.

When he is ready, he turns towards her, huge and domineering. "Omega."

"Yes?" she whispers.

"My phone."

Scowling at him, she unwraps the sheet, and collects the device from the drawer where she's locked it away. As she hands it over, his fingers brush hers and he jolts, his touch lingering for longer than it should. And then he leaves.

CHAPTER THREE

The ball sails high into the sky, spinning and rotating, then arching back towards the ground. He pumps his arms, thrusting his legs forward, eyes fixated on the revolving oval. His brain calculates the trajectory, deducing where the ball will land, and he sees he's not going to make it. He stretches out his arms and dives for the ground.

His body slaps down hard and he winces as he skids across the wet surface, forcing his eyes open, searching upwards. He spots the ball and reaches, snatching it from the air and cradling it into his body, cushioning it beneath him. Then tucking in his chin, he braces himself, his body still smarting from the impact with the pitch.

One...two...three...

Thud.

The first body hits, the weight forcing the breath from his lungs. He gasps for oxygen, hanging tightly to the ball as the man sprawling over him attempts to roll him over and prize it from his fingers. A second weight thumps on top of him, forcing his face and his body into the muddy grass, his mouth suddenly full of dirt. He swallows, forcing a breath into his crushed chest, trying not to think of the pain.

"Noah!" his team mate shouts by his ear, and gritting his teeth, he tenses his muscles and rolls, throwing the two men off his back and passing the ball. His teammate, Kyle, scoops it up and races away, and Noah clambers to his feet, spitting out dirt and breathing hard. In the distance he sees Kyle race over the line, the opposition trailing behind him.

Try.

The ref blows his whistle.

He jogs over to slap Kyle on the back.

"Good move." Kyle grins at him, the corner of his lip swollen from an earlier elbow.

"Can I take the conversion?"

Kyle shakes his head. "Coach said Harry."

"Right." He turns away quickly and sprints to the other end of the pitch, his eyes scanning the crowd as he does, his nose analysing the scents. There's a good turn out, but he doesn't see his parents. His dad had said he'd try and make the match but he hasn't heard from him today.

He keeps searching. Half way along the lines of seats he halts.

For a moment he thought... but it's not. Similar long brown hair and willowy figure.

He kicks at a tuft of grass with the toe of his boot.

For that split second he thought it was her: Cora Swift. But there's no reason she would be here, no possibility she'd come to watch him play. A girl like that is not interested in a boy like him.

She's beautiful, smart and real. More real than any girl he's met before. Fiery and sharp. Sniping and slicing her way through life and taking no prisoners.

Smelling like some heaven-sent little snack. Sexy as hell with her peach-shaped arse, long legs and sweet tits. Yet unattainable, completely unattainable, and entirely out of his league.

Not that he cares. There's a whole gaggle of girls crowded in the front rows of the stands, cheering the team's every move, squealing with delight whenever he or one of his teammates makes a tackle or scores a try. Yeah, it isn't like he is short of offers. The long list of girls in his phone, any one of them willing to be his plaything for the evening, confirms that.

But it pisses him off.

Mainly it is the way Cora looks down her nose at him as if he stinks of shit, as if she believes he isn't even worthy enough to lick the boots she walks in. He knows what she thinks of him. Same as everyone else. Dumb, rich Alpha; spoilt and entitled.

She is so stuck up, so holier than thou. Always in the right. Never in the wrong. Always making the best choices and never fucking things up.

Yeah. Not like him. He has the fantastic ability to mess everything up.

And he's done it again.

He'd not quite believed his luck when he'd stepped into the library that night and smelled her — in heat. And then she looked at him with the hint of want in her eyes. An almost inconceivable invitation.

But if he thought it would be his chance to win her over, his opportunity to change her mind, he'd been wrong. He'd mucked it up as always. And, anyway, she'd turned out to be even more of an uptight bitch than he'd realised.

He hunches over his knees and watches in the distance as Harry sets up the ball and paces backwards. It's straightforward. Anyone could make it. He could do it with his eyes closed.

The ref blows his whistles and Harry runs towards the posts, swinging back his leg and sending the ball looping through the goal. The Oxford crowd cheers and the score on the board ticks over.

Why does he care if she is here? He didn't invite her. In fact, they've not spoken since he stormed out. They've actively avoided each other, and yet he sees her everywhere. Whenever he sets foot in the library she's there studying, when he heads into a cafe to grab a coffee she's there behind the counter, when he goes for a run he finds he's passing her on the path.

He smells her everywhere too. Her scent so distinctive, so vivid, so clear above all the other lingering and intermingling odours.

It's driving him wild.

Especially when his mind keeps wandering like it does now; back to those two days they'd spent together. Every time he catches a glimpse of her, and every time he catches a whiff of her scent. Minute flashes. The skin across her back goose bumping as he sucked her gland. A dark blush rushing along her neck as she came. Her bottom lip sucked in behind her teeth, her eyelids fluttering, the skin of her nipples creasing and hardening.

He puffs out his cheeks, blowing those thoughts away, focussing back in on the game.

The ball's booted back to the centre and the teams take their positions. He grits his teeth. Another toot of the whistle and the other players throw the ball to one another as they progress onto the Oxford half.

He watches the man he's been assigned to mark, number twelve, a squat Beta who's surprisingly quick. He's positioning himself ready for a receive. Noah tracks him, prowling closer, staying just clear of his eyeline. His man darts forwards and the ball cruises back towards his waiting arms.

Noah doesn't wait. He doesn't give him time to set up the next pass. He launches at him, driving his shoulder into the number twelve's gut, hitting him hard and sending them both crashing into the mud. Harry's there straight away, snatching the ball from the opposition before they have time to react and sprinting back towards the other try line.

The number twelve swears loudly and shoves

at Noah's shoulders, but Noah presses him down harder into the ground, keeping him pinned and snarling at him. He takes his time getting up to his feet.

The man mutters something under his breath as he trots away and Noah glances over to see where the ref is, then picks up his feet, knocking against the other player as he sprints past.

"Watch it you cunt!" he growls at him.

There's only a few minutes left on the clock. His team is gaining on the line. He sprints to help, taking a quick ball and throwing it onwards. Kyle dashes it under the posts as the clock ticks over and the ref ends the game.

A win.

The atmosphere in the showers is jubilant. Someone passes around a bottle of warm champagne. Kyle tips most of it over Harry's head and then sprays foam at Noah. He lunges for him good-humouredly, and they skid around the wet bathroom floor.

It feels good to win. The other team, York, had beaten them comfortably last year, and he's pleased he pushed himself hard and helped seal the win.

After they're dressed and the coach finishes the debrief and cool down, they hit the sports bar on the Cowley Road and start on the beers. A couple of hours later someone suggests a house party further up the road with the lure of hot girls, free alcohol and maybe some coke.

As soon as he steps through the front door, he knows Cora's there. It's not just her scent, he has a sense she is, he just knows, and the dullness from the alcohol suddenly dissipates. It's like he's back on the pitch, everything heightened, everything focussed. He scans the living room. The lights are out and someone's lit candles all around the room, shadows flickering along the walls and smoke curling in the air, along with the acidic aroma of weed.

They head past a couple of other rooms, one where the music is rowdier and people are dancing, another where it seems a halfhearted game of poker is taking place, and into the kitchen. It's a large room with a long table and a crowd gathered around it. That's where she is, deep in conversation, her whole body passionately emphasising whatever point she's making.

The first time he'd seen Cora had been in the lecture hall, sat alone in the middle of a row. She had the physique of someone who'd spent most of their adolescence running and she was stretching like a cat, her arms extended above her, arching her back and rolling her head. Except it hadn't really been cat-like, there was nothing domestic about her. He knew that from the start.

Of course he'd already smelled her. Starting university had reminded him of the time his parents had taken him to a theme park and sensory overload had struck him, leaving him unsure what pleasure, what ride, to pursue first. He'd simply stood there for ten minutes, frozen with indecision, while his parents waited impatiently for him to decide

That first moment on campus had hit him in the same way. There'd been so many new scents that day, such variety. It had ignited every nerve of the Alpha inside him, giving him this jolt of energy that pounded through his body. All sorts of smells: earthy, chemical, delicate, vivid, exotic, tame, wet. And obviously among them had been hers. A scent that had tweaked his subconscious without him even mentally acknowledging it. And then in the lecture hall it was there again.

He'd watched her from the back row, entranced, absorbed by the eagerness with which she made notes, the excitement that raced through her body, the confident manner in which she raised her hand and clarified a point. To him she seemed fearless, never shying away from sharing her opinion, or arguing her side. Not like him. His brain seemed to turn to slop in those moments. His tongue heavy and slow, his mind needing time to mull things over.

He watches her again now from the corner of his eye, engaged with passion in the debate taking place, leaning right forward, her hands swirling wildly in the air around her, her brow pulled tight, every eye around the table locked on her. So different from their conversations in her bed when her hands had been tense, and her words came reluctantly.

He spots the moment she senses him, although perhaps she'd already had an inkling, her body stiffening ever so slightly like before and her eyes flitting to meet his for the briefest of moments. It electrifies every nerve in his stomach and he has to force himself to look away, not to stand there gaping at her like the idiot he is.

"Noah!" Kyle calls from the fridge as he chucks a can of lager at him. He catches it with one hand and strolls over. Mo and Harry have their arms wrapped around each other's necks and are singing some dirty song at the top of their voices. Kyle cracks open his beer and knocks his tin against Noah's.

"Shut up, will you!" shouts someone from the table. Noah spins around. Cora's gone. It's one of the men she hangs out with. Zach, isn't it? The man glares right at him, and Noah feels his blood boil.

Why is the guy looking at him like that? He draws himself up and takes a menacing step forward.

"What the fuck d'you say?" he snaps and instantly he smells the tension in the room shift.

Kyle lays a hand on his shoulder, but he shakes it off. He's glaring down at Zach so hard he feels the strain in his eyes. He can't help it. He hates him, hates the way somehow he is deemed worthy of Cora's company and attention while she won't even look at him, hates the way he recognises his scent so often mixed with hers.

The fingers by his sides are itching for a fight, an excuse to smash this man to smithereens, but then Kyle intervenes.

"Hey, guys, we won. Did you hear? Thoroughly crushed York." He lifts his can in toast and with that action the tension melts away.

There's cheering from the table and the singing restarts, moving to something less offensive, something about crushing the opposition. Zach throws Noah one more disgusted look and turns back to the small girl to his left, Cora's housemate.

Kyle pulls Noah away and he's thankful for it. Any longer and he might've been tempted to hit the self-righteous dick. He concentrates on his breathing, but Cora's scent still lingers in the room and he huffs through his nostrils, trying to drive it away.

"Let's go somewhere else," he whispers into Kyle's ear. "It's lame in here."

Kyle nods and they head to the room with the dancing. Immediately Kyle's pulled away by someone Noah doesn't know and he leans against the wall sipping his lager, eyes flicking around the room. They land on a girl he's talked to a couple of times. She spots him too and smiles at him through her fake eyelashes. He quirks his head and she walks over, hips swaying. She's cute. Big blue eyes and even bigger tits.

When she reaches him, she rests her hand on his arm and stands up on her toes to kiss his cheek, her mouth sticky with lipstick.

"Hey you," she says, her hand still on his arm, squeezing his bicep.

"Hi." He doesn't remember her name. It doesn't matter. Her perfume is strong and floral. It invades his nasal passage and wipes away all other aromas and with it all other thoughts.

She goes to say something, then hesitates, beckoning him down, and he lowers his head so she can speak in his ear, his face hovering above her cleavage.

She's telling him some story but he's already lost the thread of it. She giggles, moving closer towards him, her other hand twisting a piece of hair around and around her fingers and her body pressing into his. His hand floats down to rest on her hip. There's more to her than Cora. He can't feel the outline of her hip through her curves. If he fucked her he'd have to grip her by the flesh and not by the bone. He liked the way Cora's hip bone fit so perfectly in his hand. He liked the way she wanted to be held there. He likes the sleek lines of her.

But she doesn't like him. She can't even stand to be in the same room as him. A spike of irritation flashes through him and he bends down to mash his mouth hard onto the girls, gripping her tight. She likes it, whimpering filth about Alphas into his ear.

That's all he is to these people. An Alpha. There're girls like this one, who want an Alpha, who want him for his body. And then there are girls like Cora who hate everything he is.

He tries to home in on the sensation of the girl's lips against his, the subtle way she grinds her groin and the little whimpering noises of arousal she's making. They sound fake. Designed for his benefit.

She tastes all wrong and he can't get a grip on her odour. It's buried beneath the manufactured scents she's sprayed herself in, something he's sure the cosmetic companies claim Alpha's find irresistible.

It's nothing like Cora's scent. A scent you couldn't create or capture in a bottle. It's multi-layered and intricate. An aroma that matches what she is. Fierce, fruity and beautiful.

He catches a hint of it now. Where is she? Have his thoughts pulled her towards him? Her scent filters into the room, clear above the sticky smell of alcohol and the other girl's perfume. Cora's scent betrays her emotions, as always. Her tension, her hatred, but there's more this time. A hint of arousal. That can't be right, can it?

He leans away from the other girl and searches for Cora. She's out in the corridor, wrapped in her coat, perfectly still in the shadows, watching him. It's like that time in the library, unsaid words tripping in the air between them.

Arousal? Does she want him? He opens his mouth to call to her, then stops. Her eyes roam his face, her pupils blown wide, and he's frozen by it.

Then the other girl tugs at him and Cora averts her gaze, hurrying away. Has he screwed up again?

He's not even sure how. She confuses the hell out of him.

"You want to come back to mine?" the girl asks, her hands everywhere. He peels them from him and pushes her away.

"No." Time to leave. Perhaps he can catch up with Cora.

"What's your problem?" the girl hisses, hands on her hips, pouting like she wants him to know what he'll be missing.

He just shakes his head and leaves. Out in the cold, he hunts for Cora's scent, beginning to follow her trail. But the urgency of his steps fades as he walks down the Cowley Road, away from the bustling bars and back toward the silent city. His head thumps and his muscles are stiff from the game. At Magdalen Bridge he stops, peering down into the black river. Voices echo eerily from under the bridge and water sloshes against the stonework.

He keeps walking through the main Oxford city drag until he reaches the cross roads. He stops. Turn left and follow her scent? Turn right and head to his room? He swings his head from side to side. Then his shoulders drop and he slinks down the hill away to his place.

Three days later, he's jogging around the perimeter of the university parks when he freezes. Slowly, he twists his head to his left and then his right. He sniffs the air, chasing the molecules jostling in the breeze. It's faint, ever so faint, and he hardly believes what his brain is telling him:

Cora's going into heat. Only just — the sweet hint of it probably only obvious to someone who knows her scent so well.

He hunches over his knees, sweat running down his chin and dripping onto the pavement below. It's early. There's only been two months since her last one, when they were together. Usually Omegas only have them twice, maybe three times a year, if they're on suppressants that is and almost all Omegas are. There's a few mother-earth hippy types that don't believe in them, but they usually live on communes with hoards of babies. Clearly Cora is not one of them.

Maybe he's wrong.

He takes a long inhale through his nose, closing his eyes and focusing all his attention on the air rushing along his nasal passages, over his tongue and down his throat. There's no doubting it and there's no way in hell she's having a heat without him.

CHAPTER FOUR

Cora can't understand it. She flicks through the pages, counting the days, and then pulls out her packet of suppressants from her purse to re-examine them. They are meant to help her regulate her heats, without them she'd have one every month. Did she forget to take some? Did she count the days wrong? How can she be about to start a heat so soon after the last one?

Not that she's one hundred percent certain that she is, but there's all the usual little signs. Her sense of smell has gotten more acute, she'd retched at some man's aftershave when she'd served him coffee earlier today, and her skin is tingling, her woollen cardigan irritating her neck and wrists. Plus her mind seems a bit foggy — twice she'd given customers the incorrect change at the cafe and once she'd messed up an order.

She pulls on her coat and packs her stuff back into her bag. Explaining that she's going to need some time off can wait another day until she's certain. Hopefully someone will swap shifts with her because she can't afford to lose the money.

When she steps out onto the wet pavement,

Noah's there hovering by the doorway, his hoodie pulled up over his head, his hands buried in his coat pockets. The wind blows from the north and the cold is biting. For a split second she wonders why he is there, who he's waiting for. Then she realises he's waiting for her.

"You're going into heat?" he says with a growl, his gaze fixed on her black boots.

Well now she knows that she must be, although how the hell he sensed it when she's barely realised it herself is beyond her comprehension.

"Yes, maybe, I'm not sure. Not that it's any of your business." She begins walking and he strolls along beside her.

"I can see you through it." He's still not looking at her and his posture seems stiffer than usual. "Like last time."

"Because that was so nice!" she says.

"Yes, it was."

She looks at him in astonishment. He left her before it was over, and as shitty as that was for her, it would've been unpleasant for him too seeing as he was still in rut, still permanently engorged and hardened. How could he describe that as nice?

"It really wasn't."

"Anyway," he stops walking and she does too, unable to resist hearing what he has to say next. "It makes no difference to me. I'm offering my help if you want it, there's no need to be so catty." He holds out a scrap of paper.

"It doesn't matter either way. My house mate

will be home. I'm going to have to go it alone."

"Can't you tell her to piss off for a few days?"

"No."

His face is as taut as his body, like he's keeping a tight rein on it and any moment it might snap. It makes her edgy, and a tiny bit curious. She wonders what she'd have to do for him to break. He presses the note into her hand, quickly, before she has a chance to refuse it.

"In case."

Later, in her room, she unfolds the scrunched up note and spreads it out flat on her mattress. He's written his name (his first, no surname) and his number. She ought to throw it away. Instead, she types it into her phone. Under Jack Black. Just in case.

She'd meant to tell Rose all about it, she really had, how somehow she'd ended up in bed with Noah Wood. Over Christmas and into the new year, her thoughts and emotions had been a tangled web of self-disgust, bitterness and longing. She'd wanted, no needed, someone to confide in, someone who would help her sort through this confusion of feelings. Someone who would tell her to forget Noah Wood and the way he'd made her feel. Someone who would remind her of all the things she stood to lose if she finished up a casualty of his destruction.

Rose seemed the perfect person, actually the only person, to whom she could confess. They'd met the day Cora had arrived at Duke's College (one of the many colleges that made up part of the University of Oxford). Rose was there already, unpacking suitcases in the room they were to share. Up on the top floor of the ancient stone building, their individual bedrooms had been tiny, barely big enough for the narrow single beds, but the shared lounge had a view over the neatly kept grass of the quad on one side and the bustling streets of the city centre on the other.

They'd spent their days together, curled up on the window seat reading, writing essays and observing all the students coming and going into the college. On clear nights, when they'd been sure nobody was about to see, they'd climbed out of the windows and sat out on the roof of the college, hidden by the tall turrets that ran the perimeter of the building and gazed up at the stars discussing everything from politics to sex to their dreams for the future.

Rose was the kind of passionate individual who swept you along in the tide of their enthusiasm. Her eagerness had been infectious. American, easy going and oblivious to the hidden British snobbiness that seemed to infect so much of this new city, this new hierarchy, this new social construct, she'd shown Cora that being smart and owning an opinion could be an advantage, a tool to implement change. Without her, Cora would have been intimidated and lost, bobbing along but never brave enough to truly swim.

They rented a college flat together down a city

back road in their second year and stood for positions on the College Student Union, Rose encouraging Cora to commit her ideas in writing and submit them to the student newspaper.

Yes, Rose was the person she desperately wanted to speak to and for days before she was due to arrive back from the States, Cora had rehearsed in her head how she would explain it, how she would say it. But then Rose walked through the door, drained and exhausted, heading straight for her bedroom and flinging herself on the mattress.

"Rose, what's wrong?" Cora had asked.

"Nothing, I'm tired."

Cora followed her into the bedroom. "Didn't you sleep on the flight?"

"I haven't slept in weeks," she said into the bed.

"Why? Has something happened?"

Rose had leaned up on to her arms, puffing up the pillow and tucking it under her chin. "My parents are getting a divorce."

"What?"

Rose's family had always appeared to be a model of domestic perfection. Happy, successful, together — Rose, her mother and her father. Rose's parents had visited twice during their first year at University, insisting Cora join them for dinner, talking brightly about their lives, interested in the girls.

Rose had sighed. "It gets worse."

"What do you mean?"

Rose turned her face towards the wall.

"My bastard father has run off with another woman. A woman who's only a few years older than us."

Cora hadn't known what to say. It seemed impossible. Utterly impossible.

"Oh, and instead of doing the right and honourable thing, he's trying to screw my mom over. She's a mess." Her body had shaken then, and Cora knew she was crying. She'd lain down alongside her and wrapped her in her arms. "I've been trying to help her the best I can. With the legal stuff. It was so hard to leave her Cora."

It hadn't been the right time to reveal her own trivial, crappy concerns, and as the days passed the right time had never emerged, Rose wrapped up more and more in the increasingly messy divorce.

In the end, Cora's heat falls across the weekend and she finds herself unexpectedly alone. Someone's parents are away, leaving their large house in London empty and most of her friends head there for a party. When Rose leaves on the Friday afternoon, Cora pleads illness — what with her feverish appearance, Rose doesn't argue it. Cora's too embarrassed to admit the truth. Usually she times her heats for the holidays when Rose will be away and doesn't have to know anything about it.

The first night isn't too bad. A combination of

painkillers, a hot-water bottle and an Alpha dildo ease the pain. By late Saturday morning, though, she's writhing in agony. Usually she gets through this, she endures it. Why does it seem so much worse this time? Maybe it's because this one has happened in such quick succession to the last, or perhaps it's knowing what this would be like if he were here.

She thinks of him standing on the pavement, with the grey sky behind him, how he'd sought her out, offered himself up to her. It's more than she can bear. Her body screams at her to get him here.

CHAPTER FIVE

His knock on the door is loud, jolting Cora out of her haze. She wraps her dressing gown around her boiling body and stumbles to the hallway, leaning against the wall for support as she does. This time he has a duffel bag with him, slung over his left shoulder.

"Alright?" he says as she opens the door.

She shakes her head, utterly relieved to see him, biting down hard on her bottom lip to stop it from wobbling.

"Come on, then." He takes her hand, slamming the door shut behind them and leading her down the hall. "Get into bed. I'll be there in a moment."

"Where are you going?"

"To put this food in the fridge."

"You brought food?" She curls up on the mattress; already his presence makes her calmer, like he's a sedative.

"Of course." He stomps away, and she hears the opening and closing of the fridge and cupboard doors. When he returns, his bag is emptied and he throws it to the floor and rakes his eyes over her.

"I got tested. You wanna see the paperwork?"

Unsure if he's serious, she peers at him through her eyelashes. "No."

He nods, shrugs off his coat, and tugs his jumper and his t-shirt over his head. The February day is another dull one, and everything in the room appears muted. Except him, his skin as translucent as ever. The crisscross of his veins visible beneath his skin and dark moles scattered across his body like someone flicked him with a paintbrush. His chest and his arms are strong and defined. It's a strange combination; the fragileness of his flesh, the hardness of his muscles.

"You still sure about this, Omega?"

Why is he hesitating? He hadn't last time — he'd been unable to hold back. This time she could almost mistake his behaviour for nerves.

She lifts her head. "Do you want me to beg or something? Is that what this is?"

"This isn't anything," he says crossly and steps inside the room. She can smell him, how hard he must be, and that point somewhere deep in her abdomen buzzes with excitement. He closes his eyes and takes a deep breath in, like a smoker taking a longed for drag on a cigarette.

"What's wrong then?"

His eyes are still closed. "If we do this, I'm not sure I'll be able to stop."

What does he mean by that? She doesn't know and she remains silent, a little scared, a little delighted by the possibilities. He takes her lack of response as confirmation to proceed and whips off his jeans and boxers, stalking towards her.

Kneeling up on the bed, he pushes her down and raises her hips, guiding her on to him. He pauses to arrange a pillow under her backside and to run his hands over each of her breasts. Then he fucks her, grasping her waist and working her onto him.

As she tumbles from one orgasm to the next, she wonders vaguely how he knew that this would work. How many times he's done it before. How many women he's slept with. The boyfriend she'd been with before seems so tame in comparison to Noah. That sex had been respectful, at times tender even, but mostly perfunctory. The handful of other short dalliances and one-night stands she's had were mostly awkward and frustrating. Certainly no more satisfying than her own fingers and imagination.

With Noah, it's different. There's this rawness to him. He doesn't care what people think of him. He's not bound and limited by that, and so he unleashes everything, taking her higher than she's ever been and letting her float there, free.

Gritting his teeth, he stops himself from coming and arranges them on the bed so both have their own space. Then he releases his breath with a hiss through his teeth and she feels him flood inside her.

Although entwined together, they don't speak, but he holds her gaze until his eyelids gradually fall shut and his breathing mellows into sleep. She watches him. His face becomes more expressive as he sleeps, his brow furrowing and his mouth twitching. He's dreaming. She wonders what about. He doesn't seem the type to be haunted by nightmares.

Not like her. There's one repeating dream that's always plagued her. Pulling her back to that moment when they took her away. In her mind, she's divided everything into before that moment and after. It is puzzling to her that her subconscious should find that particular moment so distressing when the time before was clearly so much worse in so many ways than the time afterwards.

She doesn't want to think about that now, though, and ruin the pleasant haze that bathes her body. So she reaches out and traces along the ridge of his pectoral muscles and the faint lines of his abdominals, visible every time he inhales. His eyelids flutter as she does and he murmurs. His face stills and she falls asleep too.

In the afternoon, he wakes her with a glass of water and a bowl of macaroni cheese he's heated in the microwave. Her cunt throbs and she pushes the drink and the food away, reaching for him. He grasps her hands in one of his with a shake of his head.

"You need to eat and drink, Omega. I'm not fucking you again until you have." She scowls at him and his brow becomes heavy, a low guttural growl forming in his throat. "Do as you're told for once, will you?"

With a sulk on her lips, she snatches the glass from his hands and drains the lot.

"Good," he says. "Now the food." He holds out the bowl.

She turns her face aside and folds her arms over her chest. "I'm not hungry." She can't quite believe he actually cares enough to make her eat. He's here for the sex.

"Omega." His voice is stern. "You need to eat. You haven't eaten since I've been here."

She flips back around to him. "It hurts. I don't need food... you know what I do need." Her tone starts snarky, but it fades to a whimper and his face softens.

He takes her hand. She tries to pull it away but he hangs on to it firmly, pulling it towards him. Ducking his eyes to hers, he says, "I know little Omega. But just a few mouthfuls." He dips the fork into the pasta and lifts it up towards her lips. "Please."

She opens her mouth automatically, her heart swelling involuntarily at his soft words. Nobody has ever really cared whether she's eaten before. The gnawing feeling of an empty stomach is all too familiar to her.

His face stays neutral as he tips the pasta into her mouth, but she can see the strain on her forehead and around his neck, as if he's concentrating.

When she's chewed and swallowed, he offers her another mouthful and then another.

"Enough," she says after the third.

"No, Omega, all of it."

She shifts on the mattress, then nods curtly, and he feeds her the rest. He does it with patience, despite the rich aroma of her slick building in the air, and what she can tell is his growing hardness. He doesn't rush her, he takes his time, watching her lips as she chews.

"On my face, Omega," he tells her when she has eaten it all and whimpers with the returning pain.

"What?"

He lies down flat on his back and gestures to her. "On my face. I'm going to eat you out."

She shivers with the filthiness of it but does as he says. She'd probably do anything he asked. She finds she likes the thrill of being ordered about by him.

Gripping the headboard, she hovers above his face and he leans up and swipes along her swollen seam with his tongue, swirling around her entrance and back to her clit where he flicks at her viciously until her thighs shake and he has to hold her aloft to stop her from suffocating him.

In the past, there was no way she'd let a man do this to her. One or two have offered, but the thought of being so closely examined down there has had her writhing in embarrassment and shame. She feels none of those things now. Just a mind blowing ecstasy as he laps at her with all the enthusiasm of a hungry wolf.

After she comes, she scurries down his body to ride him, something else she's never done before. Reckless to it all.

Later they talk.

"Why'd you say what you did last time?" he asks. She's lying with her back against him. Maybe it's easier to talk like this, when they don't have to look at each other.

"What do you mean?"

"That stuff about me not caring about other people. Is that really what you believe?"

"Yes." She pauses. "You gonna tell me that you do — that you do the shopping for little old ladies, cut the grass at the old folks' home?" She laughs.

"You form opinions about other people very easily. What can you know about me? We don't hang out."

"I've been in the college bar when you're there with your rugby team. Seen the way you give other people a hard time, tease them, harass them."

"That's bollocks."

"No, it's not. You sit around playing your drinking games and singing your misogynistic songs and it's horrible — especially the things you chant about Omegas."

"It's a bit of harmless fun. It doesn't mean anything," he says.

"It's intimidating and hurtful and it shouldn't be allowed on campus," she snaps. In fact, she's started a campaign with Rose to get such behaviour banned from the student bar. "How do you think it makes girls feel? Fun my arse!"

He rolls away from her and sits on the edge of the bed, his feet hitting the ground with a violent thud.

"You never made a mistake, I suppose?" he mutters.

"Me?" She twists to look at him.

"Never been in trouble, I bet. Never put a foot wrong."

She stares at him in disbelief. "I can't afford to."

She learnt that very early on. She'd seen what happened to the Omega girls who did make mistakes. To the ones who got wrapped up in the gangs who ran the estates where she'd lived, and to those who'd been wooed by older men with gifts and false promises. It hadn't ended well for any of them. She knows all about that. She was nearly one of them.

"Do you have any idea how precariously I'm clinging on here?" she says, and she hears the choke in her voice, wishing it wasn't there. "One slip up, one mistake, if my grades decrease just a little, and I lose my scholarship and my grant." She tips her chin upwards and tries to calm her breathing.

It's the truth and it's hanging over her constantly like an axe about to fall. It's always there, but she's never, ever acknowledged it out loud to anyone before. He has it so easy and it's so unfair. It makes her angry, and she knows deep down it's why she hates him so much. She lowers her head and glares at him.

"It's bizarre how much you seem to hate people who try to do the right thing, seeing as it's what your mum does," she says and she can sense he's thinking about that, he examines his hands intently and his jaw works, but he doesn't answer. Finally she adds. "Did you tell anyone about last time?"

"No."

She nods and hesitates. "I don't want anyone to know."

She hears him swallow.

"Why?"

"It would be too weird. I...." She trails off, her cheeks burning, not wanting to admit the truth to him.

"It's fine," he grunts. "I don't exactly want everyone knowing I've fucked some frigid Omega."

She laughs. He can't really mean that, not after what they've done together.

"Is it like this when you sleep with other Omegas?"

He shrugs. "Pretty much." And she's surprised to find her heart sink.

On the Monday morning she hurries him out, although she has a strange sense that he's reluctant to leave. It must be his Alpha pride, wanting everything on his terms. Probably he considers being bossed about by an Omega humiliating.

On the doorstep he lingers and turns to face

her, picking at the peeling paintwork on the door frame with his thumb nail.

"What I said about this being the same as other Omegas wasn't true. I don't know why I said that. Sex has always been...." He pauses trying to find the words and a chunk of white paint flicks into the air. "At school it was something you were expected to do, you know, unless you wanted people to say you were weird. So I did and it's kind of like having an itch, you scratch and then you're satisfied and the urge goes away for a bit." He peers up at her, elevated in the hallway. "This thing between us feels different."

It's the most he's ever said to her. The most she's ever heard him say. Her mouth goes very dry and her tongue seems heavy. When she speaks, it's a strangled squeak. "Yes, it's different for me too."

The muscles on either side of his forehead tense. "Then next time you're in heat...."

She nods. He leans a little forward and she thinks he might kiss her. When he doesn't, turning away instead, she releases her breath in a sigh of relief.

She mulls over his words as she strips the soiled sheets from the bed and scrubs the mattress. She considers them as she removes the evidence of their meals to the outside dustbin and washes up the plates and cups. She thinks about them in the shower as she lathers her skin and rinses her hair.

Rose returns early in the afternoon. "You look much better," she says.

CHAPTER SIX

They see each other again, share another heat in the Easter break, then once right at the start of the summer vacation and once at the end.

In between they don't speak, they barely acknowledge each other's existence.

Sometimes he'll go to the cafe where she works and she'll serve him coffee silently.

Once he sat next to her in a lecture, and his leg pressed against hers as they diligently made notes.

Another time, he sat at the edge of a Junior Common Room meeting and listened to her speak about boosting the college's efforts to improve access for students from disadvantaged backgrounds.

In late September he returns to Oxford and the weeks pass in a tangle of training sessions, reading, matches, parties and essay writing.

Then it's early November

His practice session finishes just as the sun sets behind the outline of the city and the overhead lights snap on, flooding the pitch with white light. The other players collect up the cones and drift back to the clubhouse.

"You coming?" Kyle calls to him.

"No, I'm going to stay and kick a few penalties."

Kyle grins at him. "You're determined to get picked for it, aren't you?"

Noah nods.

"See you at the house, then." The University has a couple of houses on the Iffley Road for those who've made it onto the Varsity rugby team. He's sharing one with Kyle and four other men.

"Not until later." He groans. "I'm meeting my Mum for dinner."

"Too bad, man." Kyle chuckles. "Harry's organising a game of poker" Kyle waves at him and jogs away.

Noah carries the bag of balls to the line. His hair and his kit are damp with sweat from the training session, and the wetness quickly turns cold in the crisp temperature. He shivers against it. Then blows on his hands and jumps up and down on the spot, kicking his heels up off the ground and driving his knees towards his chest, trying to get the blood pumping around his body again.

When he's a little warmer, he places the balls out along the chalked line and concentrates on kicking each one over the bar. After each kick, he moves to the next ball along the line to try from a different angle, concentrating on adjusting his body, remembering how, when he kicks with that swing of his leg or that part of his foot, it sails through the sky — too low, or too high, to the left or to the right.

When he's kicked all the balls, he sprints behind the goal line and boots them all back onto the pitch, then starts over again. He's just preparing to kick the first ball of the second batch when Cora appears, jogging around the perimeter of the pitch out towards the towpath. She slows down, clearly watching him. It's not the first time he's seen her out here. It can't be a coincidence.

He ignores her, although her hot critique as he positions himself and hammers the ball through the twin goalposts, has the hairs peppering his spine standing on end and the palms of his hand suddenly damp.

He moves along to the next ball, wiping his hands on his shorts. Training like this, finessing his actions, perfecting his skills, has always been exhilarating, a place to pour all the untameable energy that courses through his body. He's always found it satisfying, better even than sex.

Sex has never been anything special. He's never understood why everyone else makes such a fuss about it. He knows he's good at it (what Alpha isn't?). He knows he's desired. He knows it'll never be something he really likes. Until now.

Because he likes it with her. He can't help it. Her body is like a drug he can't get enough off, one he keeps returning to again and again. Everything about her is a temptation. He likes the way she smells and how it makes the gland at the back of his neck tingle. Likes the earthy way she tastes. Likes the soft feel of her supple skin. And the long strangled groan she makes whenever she comes.

It's embarrassing to like these things, to need them so much and so badly. Shameful. A truth he doesn't want anyone else to know about. His sex life is usually a topic he dissects with his team mates. His time with Cora feels private and intimate, as if he's shown more of himself than he'd like to, and it won't be something he'll be sharing.

He can see her from the corner of his eye as he kicks again, her gaze eating him up as she circles the pitch like a tiger nearing his prey. He'd happily be caught, he'd happily be eaten, he'd happily surrender himself to her. But she never comes any closer and when he tries to call out to her, he finds the words won't come. Eventually she swerves off down the path and he loses her behind the tall firs.

It's for the best. He needs to get changed and go meet his mother. His body slumps at the thought and he gathers up the balls and stuffs them into the oversized bag, slinging it over his shoulders. The clubhouse is empty when he enters, and his hand pats along the wall until he finds the light switch. He dumps the bag in the store cupboard and heads to the changing room. It's empty too, although the scents of his teammates still hang in the air. Aggressive mixtures of sweat, testosterone and spunk. He snorts and wipes his nose between his fingers.

In the shower, he realises he didn't have to wait there for her. He could have been the one to catch her, to drag her into the shower with him, to push her up against the tiles and have her.

He rubs the shampoo into his scalp with force, his short nails scratching at the skin, then twists the knob to freezing and forces himself under the water, wincing against the cold, his chest tightening and his breath sharp.

Why does she ignore him? What is it about him that means she's happy for him to fuck her but she doesn't want to be seen with him, can barely bring herself to look at him when there's other people around?

The shampoo runs down his face, white foam swimming over his torso and slopping onto the ground. He pumps at the shower gel and scours his body with it, scrubbing away the mud and the sweat and the grime, working at his skin so hard it's almost painful.

His mother is waiting for him in the restaurant, already at a table in the corner with two younger women he suspects are from her office, one either side. It disappoints him — he'd hoped he'd have her to himself — and so he's glad that he's late. Tardiness has always displeased her.

Her eyes flip to him as he arrives and she waves him towards a seat at the other side of the table, continuing to nod as she listens to the colleague on her right, a tall slender woman with hair twisted into a bun and red glasses that match her lipstick. The other woman is rounder with big curly hair. Both wear tight fitting dresses while his mother is dressed in a blouse and trouser suit. He feels underdressed in his dark jeans and black shirt.

Ignoring her gestured instruction, he leans over the first woman to kiss his mother but she draws away from him.

"Don't lean over Liz like that Noah. You'll squash her." she laughs shrilly and flaps her hand at him, shooing him away.

"Sorry," he mumbles, folding into the chair and picking up the menu, examining it intently.

"You're late," his mother says, "so I ordered for you."

Placing the menu down on the table, he flattens his hands on its surface, spreading his fingers.

Their conversation resumes and he sits there silently, listening to them discussing how a case to alter the rights to divorce is proceeding through the High Court. At one point, the woman with the glasses turns to him and asks, "What do you think Noah?"

He can tell she's trying to be kind, that she's aware of his awkward bulk quietly listening, but inwardly he groans.

What does he think? What does he ever think? The thoughts in his head are always so muddled and confused, fogged by the ever present scents swirling in the air, bullied by the basal instincts he possesses to speak with his fists. He wants to home in on their words and their ideas, but the aroma of cooking meat from the kitchens, the scent of a mated couple becoming ever more aroused at the table next to them, the assaulting stink of the scented candles burning along the windowsill, and his mother's peaking tension, all compete for his attention, dragging his mind in different directions.

He drums his fingers on the table and looks away to the window where the Oxford streets are bustling with people. "I don't know," he grunts.

His mother huffs. "Noah's never shown an interest in these things, despite my best attempts. Not like his brother Charlie." She twists the stem of her wineglass in her fingers. "Did I tell you what he's working on over in New York?"

He continues to stare out the window as his mother gives her colleagues a rundown of his brother's latest achievements.

He's bored as hell. All he wants to do is pull out his phone. Instead, he waits until finally the waiter brings their food. It's steak and he passes the time by cutting it into many tiny pieces and then chewing each one. Over the table his mother frowns at him but says nothing, and he gulps down the wine. When he's done, he fiddles with his cutlery.

Finally, when the desserts arrive, his mother turns her attention to him. It's like an interrogation light swinging his way and he shrinks further into the chair, wanting to shield his face and his eyes.

"And what about you, Noah?" she says.

"What about me?"

Her lips tighten. "How're your studies?"

"Fine," he says, sweeping a strawberry backwards and forward through a wad of chocolate sauce. The sauce is too stiff and instead of slicing through satisfactorily, the strawberry is gradually mashing into mush.

"And your rugby?" His mother turns to her colleagues, "Noah's on the university rugby team."

"Wow," the woman with glasses says, leaning forward onto her elbows, running her eyes subtly down his form.

"He can never keep still." She shakes her head. "Never has been able to."

He keeps his eyes fixed on his plate, but he can hear the slight annoyance in his mother's voice. She finds his energy and his moods irritating. In fact, she's probably always found him irritating. It was a lot of 'not now's and 'Mummy's busy' growing up.

He raises his gaze. "Actually, a scout came to our game last Wednesday; from one of the premier league clubs."

"How exciting." His mother is not eating pudding; he's the only one who is. But she's ordered a coffee and raises the white cup to her mouth, leaving the burgundy imprint of her lips on the rim. His mother is very beautiful; still, even now in her fifties. She has the same caramel eyes as him, long lashes and the type of bone structure that always catches the light in the right way. With her high cheekbones and striking jawline, the creases and wrinkles on her face are easily forgotten. "Did they spot anyone?"

He coughs and wishes his father was here. They seem rarely together these days. "Me."

His mother's mouth forms a soundless 'oh' shape. "You can't be serious, darling?"

He shrugs. It had never occurred to him as a serious option before, and anyway he assumed he'd be too old for opportunities like that. But the man from the club had taken a note of his email address and said he'd be in touch about a summer training camp. He's not sure it is what he'd like to do with his future but it occurs to him it would be preferable to working in an office.

"And how about your girlfriend?"

He shoots a look at his mother, who is already waving at the waitress for the bill.

"I don't have a girlfriend."

"What happened to that girl you were seeing over the summer? I had the impression you liked her." His mouth falls open a tiny bit and he runs his tongue along the rear of his teeth. She knew about that? He'd never told her where he was going when he went to visit Cora, and he assumed she'd barely noticed his absences. But she must have smelled it on him — she is an Omega after all. Not that anyone would know. She has the petite frame of an Omega, but she acts and speaks like anything but.

He doesn't answer.

The waitress arrives with the bill, smiling coyly at him from under her eyelashes, her hand resting lightly on his shoulder as she bends over him to collect up glasses. She's an Omega and she's making it clear that she's interested. His mother scowls at him and asks for their coats stiffly. The waitress blushes and scurries away. Did he do something wrong?

When it's time to leave, his mother pats him on the cheek, swerving away for her coat as he leans down to kiss her and he steps outside onto the pavement waiting to be dismissed.

Her car is parked a few spaces down the high street, and she unlocks it with a press of the keypad. The headlights flash.

"Can I pay for a taxi home for you, darling?" she asks as the two colleagues climb into the car, one into the back and one into the passenger seat.

"No, I'll walk," he says, turning and strolling away, his hands buried deep in his pockets and his eyes stinging against the bitter wind.

Three days before they're due to break up for the Christmas holidays, Cora texts him to tell him she'll be going into heat. Her message as always is blunt and he can't help but send an equally grumpy response. The exchange that follows is terse and short, but nonetheless the tension he'd been carrying in his spine melts away, a tightness in his limbs he hadn't realised was there evaporating. He knew she'd arrange things, but there had still been this fear that she wouldn't.

CHAPTER SEVEN

Rose gives Cora department store vouchers as a Christmas gift. To Cora this is infinitely better than some hand crafted personal gift that many of her friends coo over. This gift is practical.

Even with her hardship grant and her wages from the coffee shop, she has very little spare cash and she's determined to keep her debt to a minimum. Her student loan already has her feeling sick, the numbers so phenomenally large she can't quite bring herself to believe she will have to pay that back one day. Sometimes she wakes up suddenly in the middle of the night bathed in hot sweat, her heart racing like an express train in her chest, the image of that number a ghostly image across her eyelids.

Vouchers, along with a small Christmas bonus from the cafe, means she can buy new socks and new pants.

The department store heaves, people jostling around one another, knocking each other's shins with full shopping bags, squeezing through small gaps with irritated huffs. Boppy Christmas music blasts above the noise of the beeps of the tills and the pound of many pairs of feet on the laminate floors.

This year the store has chosen a silver theme to compliment some Christmas blockbuster that was released a week ago. It was a mistake, she thinks. The store feels colder as a consequence, although in fact it's far too warm, the heaters streaming hot air over the shoppers in their heavy coats.

She hooks her own coat over her arm and takes the escalator up to the second floor and the women's underwear department. As she steps off the moving steps, she's greeted by a collection of mannequins arranged around a sofa. Two perch on the arms, one lounges across the cushions, and the final two stand against the sofa's back. All are dressed in lingerie. Skimpy, bras and knickers, or corsets, garter belts and stockings, one has a gauzy dressing gown draped over her shoulders with pom poms hanging from the ribbon belt, another wears silk French knickers with a matching camisole. The colours are deep jewels; blacks and reds and purples.

She stands and stares at them.

Cora has never liked her body. Partly because being an Omega brings discrimination and boundaries as well as the physical difficulties she has to endure, such as heats and heavy periods. Then there are the very real dangers it presents. Passing through puberty and stepping into her new body was like emerging into a new world. A more adult and frightening world where men looked at her with a sudden interest that seemed possessive and violent, and where her body responded to smells and images against her will.

She'd had to learn quickly how to navigate this new world. How to stay out of the path of Alphas, how to repress the strange desires that weren't really hers, how to keep herself safe.

But it wasn't just being an Omega that resulted in the repulsion with her body. She would've felt dissatisfied with it, even if she'd been a Beta. She doesn't possess the supple curves of the women she can see pinned to the rows of bras, smiling coyly above their cleavages. Her body is all jutting bones and lean muscle.

She's been called pretty several times over the years. Her friends say she is. She supposes maybe they are right. She has a pleasant face, unobtrusive and almost plain. She's a cartoon, not a painting. Cute, not beautiful. Button nose, round cheeks and bowed lips. The only feature she really likes are her eyes. Their colour is an icy blue — and she can use their coolness to her advantage.

Behind the harem of mannequins are the displays of underwear; there to tempt husbands and partners. It makes her smile. She can't picture Noah here searching through the bras and knickers, but she has a sudden thought that he'd like to see her dressed in them. She takes a step closer.

There's a blood red set, the bra triangular with no padding. It's transparent and she can see the nipples of the lady modelling the set. She touches it. The material is gauzy. Maybe it's her approaching heat because the thought of it against her own skin, brushing over her nipples, has excitement growing in her belly. Yes, she'd like him to see her in this. She'd like him to trace the straps with his fingertip, skate along the cups, flick open the clasp and let it trail down her arms.

No, she shouldn't spend her money on that. She needs practical knickers — the kind you can ride a bike in and run for the bus. She strolls to the aisle that houses the boxed cotton briefs. Searching through the packs, she finds her size in some plain white variety with a little bow at the front. She could purchase five of these sets for the same price as the red bra and knickers. But she doesn't own anything as pretty, as sexual, as that and she notices herself wandering back over and touching it again.

Would she look good in it? She isn't sure. Does it matter? In the end she decides to buy the set as much for herself as him.

◆ ◆ ◆

The flat is decorated with paper chains Rose crafted, and there's a string of white lights twisted around the window in the front door. Rose also insisted on buying a dwarf Christmas tree that stands in the kitchen. She clearly loves the build up to Christmas; fully embracing the playing of music, baking of cookies, wrapping of presents. She hasn't realised that Cora's lack of enthusiasm for the celebration is not down to her cynicism with capitalism, but is more to do with the fact that she'll be spending Christmas alone again. Although she hasn't told Rose or her other friends that she's staying in the flat for the holidays. They assume she has somewhere to go, and she doesn't tell them otherwise. There would probably be someone who would invite her to stay, but she hates being the charity case. She hates being reminded that she's alone.

Sometimes she feels like a boat on an ocean with no anchor. No way to stop herself from drifting aimlessly about, from crashing into rocks or being swept away in a rip tide. Other people have those anchors. They have many, as well as ropes to bind them to the shore and keep them safe.

The few times she'd gone to stay at a friend's house, she'd felt strangely removed. As if she was not possessing her body but was watching the familial scene apart from it, not really there.

Noah will be here for her heat during the first few days of the break and then he will leave too and she will occupy herself with cleaning up the mess from their time together and will forget the rest of the world is living without her.

As usual, his knock on the door is brisk and impatient and he has his duffel bag on his shoulder. She follows him through to the kitchen, keen to see what he's brought, and hovers around him as he unpacks the food items into the fridge. There's mince pies and Christmas chocolates as well as a small turkey breast and ready prepared gravy, roast potatoes and vegetables. When he's finished, he twists around.

"Your fridge is always so bloody empty," he says. "If I didn't bring you food, I'm sure you'd starve to death in your heat."

"I like that you bring me food."

He smirks. "Why?"

"I dunno." She shrugs playfully. "I could lie and say I keep the cupboards deliberately bare so you're forced to bring me food. But actually Rose does the shopping and I always forget to get food when she leaves."

He hooks a finger through the belt loop of her denim skirt and pulls her towards him. She comes willingly.

"You need to take better care of yourself, Omega." He kisses her. It's tentative, like it always is at the beginning with them. He's checking he's still welcome and tasting whether there's any unspoken resentment lingering on her lips.

Sometimes there is. Sometimes she needs to berate him for things she's heard or seen him do — she has to get that off her chest, rail at him a bit and him her in return — before she can submit herself over to her body and her needs.

But this time she's nothing to say. Now they are both living off campus she hardly sees him. The occasional shared economic lecture (he's been turning up for more of them), the odd house party, sometimes a night out at the same bar. She thinks his rugby must be keeping him busy. He's got a permanent place on the university team and is living in one of the team houses. She knows they train a lot.

Once, by coincidence, she passed him practising while out for a run, although perhaps she'd been unconsciously lured there by his scent. He smells more vivid, more concentrated and strong when he's pushing his body and his skin shines with that film of sweat. She often catches a taste of it in the air. Even when it's old and stale, she still finds herself chasing it with her mouth, enjoying the strange tingle of him on the tip of her tongue. It brings images of him, of them, and she finds her skin heating. It's strange how smells do that to her — transport her to other times and places. Often those journeys and those memories are not good. But undeniably, with his scent, it's different. It elicits pleasant feelings, and it is bitterly confusing.

She's fallen for the temptation to run that way again. He probably finds it annoying to have her hanging about conspicuously like that. Omegas and Alphas can't be seen within ten feet of one another without sparking rumours — most of them lewd and involving huge leaps towards ludicrous assumptions.

His kiss becomes more impassioned, and he

lifts her up and places her on the kitchen work-top. He sweeps aside her hair and wraps his tongue around her gland once, twice, three times. She's given up telling him to stop doing that. It feels like nothing she can describe. Heavenly, transporting, trans-lifting. She scrapes her fingernails into the wood of the countertop to stop herself from begging him to bite her there. Instead she tilts her head, allowing him to consume the sensitive spot completely. His hands stroke up the outside of her thighs and circle her waist.

When he pulls away his eyes are tender; his black pupils suspended in the molten sugar of his irises. It does something to her when he looks at her like this, with want and desire swirling across his face. It makes her want to do almost anything to get him to fuck her.

She reaches under the hem of her skirt and wriggles down her woollen tights. He trails the knuckles of his finger along the tender side of her thigh, right the way up to the gusset of her under-wear, already wet with slick. Then he removes her thick jumper and her top so she's sat in just her skirt and bra.

"Fuck," he mutters when he gets a look at the scarlet bra. His eyes widen and he stares, his eyes travelling over the rise and fall of each breast. "Fuck."

"We really shouldn't do this here," she whispers, butterflies flitting in her stomach as he shrugs off his own sweater and t-shirt, and rubs a flat palm over the rigid muscles of his chest.

"You worried the pearl clutcher will disapprove."

"No, I'm thinking more of the practicalities when we end up stuck here."

"Easy access to the fridge." He grins, showing his white slightly crooked front teeth. His hands are under her skirt, one large finger slipping under her knickers and circling her entrance. "And I'd like to fuck you here. Then every time you sit here eating dinner with your friends, you'd have to think about what we'd done." He nudges a finger inside her and strokes at the point he knows she loves.

"Noah," she gasps as she lifts open her legs to give him more room and tips her head back.

"I'll carry you back to bed." He says it in a low painful moan as his lips find her collarbone and he sweeps them wet along to the right strap of her bra. With his free hand, he cradles her shoulder and brushes the strap aside, following it with his mouth as it falls down her arm until he's at her breast. He pauses, rubbing the tip of his nose against her hardened nipple and the feel of the material and the warmth of his skin are exactly as she'd imagined.

"You know," he whispers, his breath rushing over her nipple and making her gasp. "This is the best Christmas present."

"You like it?"

"What do you think?" he says, suddenly biting

her nipple through the bra, tugging at it with his teeth. "I almost don't want to take it off. But your tits are so insanely soft." He pulls the gauze away to free her breast and rubs his cheek over the creased skin.

"Hmmm," she moans. His attention to every little part of her is always surprising. She never knew a tongue in her ear, or a stroke to the sole of her foot, or breath between her thighs could make her so alive, so desperate for more.

Slick coats his hand and he cups her, grinding the heel of his hand over her sensitive nub until she's lost to a wave of pleasure and begging him. Only then does he enter, taking a hold of her backside and plunging inside. He pauses, searching out her eyes, ensuring she's ready for him and then driving further.

Later in bed, he asks her, "Where are you going for Christmas this year, Omega?"

She doesn't answer him. It's not something she wants to talk about.

He scrubs his hand down his face, as if trying to remove some annoying thought. "Do you... would you want to come to mine?"

Her cheeks burn with embarrassment. She doesn't want his sympathy or his charity. "No," she says, finally.

He nods, thinking. "You know I'd stay with you if I could. But I can't — I have to go home. My brother is over for Christmas and my life won't be worth living if I'm not there too."

Shocked, she says, "I don't want you here."

"Right, yeah."

But when he leaves three days later, the evening before Christmas Eve, he seems to take longer than usual cleaning himself up and packing his things, and she hovers around him, sitting on the edge of the bed as he kneels on the floor and fills his bag with his clothes, leaning against the counter top as he sorts out the food in the fridge.

"I've left you the Christmas dinner, " he says.

She nods, a lump in her throat.

"I've got to go now — if I miss this train, there won't be another one for hours." He slings his bag over his shoulder and hesitates. He steps towards her and her breath catches. He cups her cheek in his hand and she steels herself. He pauses again, then brushes his lips over her forehead.

"Happy Christmas, Cora."

She closes her eyes, smelling the confusion she feels in her scent. He must smell it too. Her own hands twitch, wanting to cradle his hand in hers, wanting to push him away.

"Happy Christmas, Noah."

He withdraws his hand and walks steadily away, halting at the door. "Shit, I nearly forgot. I got you a present." He drops his bag to the floor and rummages through the pocket at the end.

"Oh, you didn't — I mean, you'll miss your train," she stutters.

Closing the distance between them quickly, he thrusts the small bundle into her hands. It's bound neatly in silver paper, but there's no tag. She tucks her thumb under a fold of the wrapping paper.

"You can't open it yet. You have to wait until Christmas day." He grins at her.

She squeezes the gift with her hands. Whatever is inside is squidgy, not solid. "Okay, but I didn't get you anything. I feel bad."

"Cora," he says, "that red underwear."

She smiles, but can't meet his meaningful look.

He hangs his bag back over his shoulder. "You know if you did want to give me something," he pauses, then finishes quickly, "you could let me have those knickers."

"But they're not washed."

The side of his mouth twitches and his eyes spark with amusement. "Cora, that's the whole point."

Heat creeps from her chest, up her throat and to her cheeks. "It's just, they cost me a lot of money."

Now his cheeks glow. It's the first time she's made him blush. "Right. Fine. You keep them then. I'd rather get to see you in them again, anyway."

She hugs her gift to her stomach and he strides down the hall, lingering at the door to peer back at her. "Take care of yourself," he says before shutting the front door.

The door slams with a thud and then it's silent, eerily silent, the flat bare and empty without his presence.

She traipses to her room, resisting the urge to

rip open his gift, and lies face down on the soiled mattress, inhaling their combined smell.

On Christmas day, she zips on the Christmas onesie Zach bought her and puts the Christmas dinner in the oven. While she's waiting for the food to cook, she unwraps his present. It's a small fluffy panda with a tag around its neck.

To keep you company, Noah x

It's the kind of thing an Omega likes — soft and snuggly against the skin. It's the kind of thing a boyfriend gives a girlfriend. It's the kind of toy you buy a lonely child.

What does it mean?

When her dinner is ready and set out attractively on her plate, she positions the panda alongside and takes a photo with her phone. She sends it to Noah with a thank you.

He doesn't respond until the evening when she's tucked up in bed eating Celebration chocolates and watching the Strictly Christmas special on her laptop.

Noah: Have you named him?

She has. It feels a little silly. She's never owned a stuffed toy before, it's always seemed a bit juvenile and, well, not very sophisticated. But he has a cute, endearing, squishy face.

Cora: Yes. But you mustn't be mean.

Noah: He's your bear. Name him exactly what you want.

Cora: His name is Confucius.

Noah: After the philosopher? You're such a nerd.

Cora: It suits him.

The next day, she snips Confucius's tag from his neck and slides it between the pages of her notebook, unsure why she doesn't place it in the bin. She considers stuffing the panda in the bottom of her wardrobe, but she can't bear to think of him all alone in the dark, and so she finds him a spot on the shelf above her desk where he can watch her work.

CHAPTER EIGHT

The phone rings six times before he picks up, six long stretches of bells ringing in her right ear followed by six excruciating pauses, her anxiety rising a little higher with every one. She chews her bottom lip and twists the middle button of her coat around and around.

Finally, there's a click at the other end and his gruff voice, a hint of surprise in his tone.

"You alright?" he says. There's the noise of traffic behind him and the chime of a bicycle bell.

"Yes." She screws shut her eyes. "I mean, not really."

"What's wrong?"

"I just had this massive row with one of my tutors."

"Isn't that what tutes are all about? Intellectual debate and—"

"No, a proper shouting match. I told her to fuck off. And now I feel — urgh." She throws back her head and watches her breath stream out in a wisp of white.

There's a pause. "And so you called me because, obviously, I'm frequently telling my tutors to fuck off." There's a trace of venom in his voice and she pulls away the phone from her ear and scowls at it as if in doing so he'll be able to see. Then she hangs up with a violent jab of her thumb.

He calls straight back. She contemplates not answering, but she needs to talk this out of her system and she wants to talk to him.

"Where are you?" he says, no apology in his voice.

"In the university parks by the big beech tree."

"I'll be there in fifteen minutes. Okay?"

"Okay."

She paces around the tree while she waits for him, trying to dispel the thundering cloud of anger brewing inside. It's late January and the park is empty. The tourists left months ago and the students are tucked up in libraries or labs studying. The soles of her trainers sink into the damp ground as she walks, and soon she's treading over her own prints, dizzy with her steps and her thoughts.

The trees are bare and they stand starkly against the pale sky. Unmoving. The stillness of the weather irritates her. It should be raging like her. Instead, it's mocking her with its calmness. She doesn't like the emotion of anger. It has always burned like a poison, one she'd like to vomit out. At times, after it's infected her body, left her shaking uncontrollably, she has. Anger is green bile in white toilet bowls.

Noah arrives pushing his bike quickly along

the gravel pathway. His face is hard, concerned but wary, and his grip on the handlebars is white knuckled. The bike is expensive, of course, shiny new paintwork, and complicated looking gears and brakes. She hardly uses her own. She picked it up at a sale of abandoned cycles the university holds at the end of each year. The rear brake came unattached last week and now she has to drag her feet along the road when she wants to slow down.

He stops several paces away from her as if he's afraid to come closer. Jerking his chin at her, he asks, "What happened?"

"It's bullshit — all such bullshit," she snaps.

He studies her. "Your tutor?"

"She slammed my essay in front of everyone, tore it to shreds. But it wasn't bad, she just didn't agree with my point of view. And I lost my temper and I know she's going to report me and then what? I can kiss goodbye to my scholarship."

"They're not going to take your scholarship away for one little indiscretion, Cora."

She glares at him. "You haven't read my scholarship agreement, Noah. You haven't seen the conditions and the rules — the expectations.

"I haven't, but they can't kick you out for that, especially when the tutor was being a dick."

She hears him, but she's too fired up to acknowledge it. "They tell you, they always tell you, that you're free to explore ideas, share your opinions. But you're not. It has to be the right ideas and the right opinions."

He nods.

"I feel," she groans, throwing her hands out to her sides, "so trapped."

He nods again, and his right thumb slides over the sticker on his handlebars. He's listening hard, she can tell that there's an intensity about his body trained on her words.

She kicks at the trunk of the beech tree, crunching the nettles growing around the base. Above them, a crow screeches. "I've always felt so confined, you know. I came here to uni and at last I felt like I'd been let out of a cage, that finally I'd been freed. But I was an idiot. I'm still trapped, the cage is just bigger with different shaped bars."

He chuckles bitterly. "The entire world's a cage, especially for people like you and me." He scratches his nail along the outline of the sticker. "What was the essay about?" Reaching into the pocket of his jacket, he pulls out a small hip flask and, flipping off the cap, passes it to her.

"Omega and Alpha rights and responsibilities."

"Let me guess: your tutor is a Beta."

She nods and takes a large gulp from the flask. The flavour is sickly sweet, and she smiles as she coughs.

"Peach schnapps? I wouldn't take you for a fruit liquor man!"

'I didn't think you'd like whiskey."

"Well, no, but rum or gin might have been better."

He grins. "I didn't think of that." He reaches

for the flask and takes a swig himself. "Shit, that's awful," he says, making a face, then shoves the flask into his pocket and tugs up the zip. "Peaches remind me of you."

"Oh yeah?" she says. Her anger is fading. She thought she'd called him to scream and shout at him, someone to let go at. Instead, his presence is calming. "You gonna say something sexist about my arse?"

He laughs, a quiet, shy sort of noise. "No. You smell faintly of them."

"Do I?"

"Yes — I can just about smell peaches above the other nasty shit."

She smiles and looks away to the ground. He's wearing black trainers, and the bike rests against his muscular thigh.

"I don't think I could describe the way you smell. Complex, maybe."

"I'm not complex. I'm simple as fuck." They both know that's not true. "Do you want to walk down to the Bell Arms? Get a drink?"

She stares at him. His expression is neutral, as ever. It's impossible to tell if he's amused or put out or wanting her company. "Yes. I want to get smashed."

"Your little friend will come and have me arrested if she thinks I've got you drunk.'

Her anger flashes suddenly, like lightning.
"Why shouldn't I get pissed? With you?"
He doesn't say anything.

"I want... I want to do whatever I want. I want to be whoever I am." She pauses and swallows slowly. "I have all this frustration, all this anger inside. But I'm not allowed to express it. I'm not allowed to be those things: angry, frustrated. Not if I want to keep my scholarship. Not if I want people to like me."

He runs his hand through his hair, pushing away the long dark tresses from his face. "You're always angry with me."

"And you don't like me."

She holds his eyes and a heat rises inside her to meet the rage. He's so magnificent, standing there, solid and unflinching, as if he has hidden roots and can't be shaken.

"I do like you."

The pub is empty. Noah chains his bike to a lamppost outside and they sit by the fire and drink pints. They talk, and after that they're friends. They meet regularly for coffee or a drink, quiet places where they won't be seen. There's an unspoken understanding between them they don't want others to know about this friendship. They want to keep it private, so he never comes to her house and she never goes to his.

CHAPTER NINE

They're friends. He isn't sure exactly how that happened, but it makes him happy. He enjoys her company. Her presence is calming, soothing, like sinking into a warm bath and letting the water dissolve away all the grime that is your life. He forgets about his anxieties and his worries when he's with her. Time actually freezes, and everything is the here and the now only.

It's bliss.

It's bliss, except for the underlying invisible line that runs beneath this friendship. Like a blood vessel; you know it's there doing its job, pumping your blood, but you can't see it with your eyes. Sometimes you sense it. Sometimes so strongly it's all you can think of. But it's never visible.

And the line is his attraction for her. Her scent alone has him hardening if he lets himself focus in on it. He forces himself not to, concentrating on her words or the parts of her with no sexual connotation. He can't look at her waist because he'll imagine his hands coiled there. He can't look at her mouth because he'll think about tugging her bottom lip between his teeth. He can't look at her thigh because he'll slip into memories about the softness of her flesh beneath the hard denim of her jeans.

It's getting more difficult. Everything about her sexualised, erotic, evocative. The tip of her shoulder, the point of her elbow, the knuckle of her fingers. He'd like to lick, suck, taste them all. He wants to love every part of her. Fuck, even her arsehole — especially her arsehole.

This meeting is the fourth time since she'd called him and he'd gone to meet her below the beech tree.

She is there first. She always is. He can't bring himself to be on time. He doesn't want her to spot his eagerness.

She's curled up on a bench seat in the corner of the pub, her feet tucked up beneath her, leaning against the chair's arm and reading a book. She's engrossed, her eyes sweeping across the page as she chews on her left thumbnail.

He halts and takes a deep breath in. For a moment, he considers walking away. Just a silly, fleeting thought. He could no more leave than he could stop breathing.

Her eyes halt and he knows she's caught his scent. They are both frozen, and he resists the urge to sniff and try to deduce what she's feeling.

With his hands stuffed in his jacket pockets, he stalks forward and she lowers her book and smiles up at him. A genuine smile, like she might actually be happy to see him.

"Hi," she says, and her voice is almost a sigh.

"Hi." He pulls out a chair and goes to sit, then remembers he needs a drink. "Can I get you anything?"

"Got one already, thanks." She points to her pint with her closed book, placing it on the dark varnished table.

It's an old man's pub. The patrons belong to the town and not the university. A couple of old boys sit on high stalls at the bar, propping up either end. One is talking to the barman as he unloads steaming glasses from a wire tray, the other has spread out his paper and studies the aggressive headlines.

Noah orders a pint of dark ale, sipping away the fine layer of creamy head as he waits for the barman to ring up the total. He taps his credit card against the contactless machine and returns to Cora.

She's so tiny, he thinks as he draws out a chair and sits opposite her. She's economical, there's no waste to her, nothing unnecessary. But she's not fragile. There's a power to her, twitching in her joints and in her muscles. He always gets the impression that at any moment she could spring into motion.

He shrugs off his jacket and takes another mouthful of drink. She smiles as she watches him, waiting for him to swallow.

"You okay then?" he asks.

"Yep."

"What you reading?"

"Just some trashy romance novel."

His mouth twitches, and he tries to cover it with his hand.

"What?" she says, smiling wider in that way that grounds him.

He can't help smirking. "You ... read romance novels?"

"Every woman reads romance novels."

"I had you marked as being into high end literature."

"Well, I like that too but sometimes I want something fun and, I don't know, happy."

"Shit." He shakes his head, returning her smile. "I'm genuinely surprised."

"You cold hearted Alphas can't enjoy a good romance?"

"Hey now," he says, his mouth twitching. "It's not what I'd choose to read or watch."

"I don't believe you've never seen a RomCom."

"Maybe, I don't remember."

She laughs at him. "You're so full of shit."

"I'm serious."

"What is your favourite film then?"

"The Departed."

She screws up her nose. "Is that that gangster film?"

"Yeah, it's brilliant."

"But really violent, right?"

"'Suppose." He pauses. "I really thought you'd be

into that sort of thing too."

"Mindless violence?"

"No, psychological thrillers, political intrigues, social commentary — that stuff. Not fluff."

"I do like that. But sometimes you need a little sweetness with your sour."

He jerks his chin at her. "What's your favourite film?"

"Hmm. Probably When Harry met Sally. I watch it quite a bit."

"I've never seen it."

"You should." She picks at the skin around her little fingernail. "We could watch it together."

The muscle beneath his eye jerks. He tries very hard not to inhale deeply and get an understanding of her intent. He fails, his nostrils flaring as he draws her scent in. She watches, very still. But her emotions are a whirr of contradictions he can't understand. "You inviting me round for a movie night?" he finally says. "I can't see your flatmate approving." There's a trace of bitterness in his voice.

"Oh no, I meant online. Virtually."

"Right." He hopes the sudden dejection isn't visible on his face. Swiftly, he reaches and lifts his pint glass to take another swig. The door to the pub opens and a man balancing a box on his shoulders struggles in, a cold wind whipping in after him.

"What did you do to your hand?" she asks, pointing to the knuckles of his left hand. They are swollen with a criss cross of brown grazes.

He flips his hand over to examine the injury as if he didn't know it was there. "Ahh, nothing."

It had happened the night before. He'd been coming home from training, wrapped up in his tracksuit with a puffer coat zipped over the top, his kit bag over his shoulders. It had been an intense session and he'd pushed himself hard. Now his skin had the salty taste of sweat and stale odour. He wanted to get to the house and take a long shower.

It was nine o'clock but the street was still busy, cars slicing through greasy puddles and the pavements full with students returning from studying, or loaded with shopping bags. Some were out for the night, obvious from their lack of coats. Wednesday night was student night at the nightclub, a long line of cold and chattering people already wound down the pavement. He passed them, mindful of the eyes that examined him as he did, conscious of a mixture of desire, jealousy and aggression hanging in the air. The hairs on the back of his neck bristled, and he walked faster, sensing some threat invisible in the line. But it was too late. The threat, three large men, clearly wasted, further up the queue, had spotted him. They were bored and frustrated — he could read it in the way they stood, in the way their eyes raked the scene, looking for excitement, searching for a fight.

"Hey Alpha!" one shouted, a squat fair man, shorter than Noah but well built. Noah kept walking, wishing he'd plugged in his earphones. "I said hey you!" The man stepped out of the line, blocking Noah's path.

He tried to remember all the things they'd taught him over the years — don't make eye contact, focus on your breathing, tune in to your senses, walk away. He tried — aware of the brightly lit bus bumbling past them on the road, of the moist air cool on his skin, of the stink of old urine permeating from the cracks in the concrete, of the whispering of anxious voices, of the taste of his own saliva on his tongue. But the smells of the threat and danger were already speaking to his Alpha — his blood pumping hot and violent through him — so he curled his hands and stared into the man's face.

"What?" he growled.

The other man planted his feet and drew up his forefinger, pointing it at Noah like a gun. "You got a problem, Alpha scum?"

Noah glared at him, his brow drawn down over his eyes. "No." He continued to walk forward. The man's friends joined him on the pavement, flanking him with sneers on their faces. One gripped a bottle half full with beer that sloshed on the floor as he moved.

He could make a swing for the first one suddenly, before he'd realised what was happening, stun him and then face the other two. He was bigger than them and his Alpha genetics gave him a strength they didn't possess. But it would be precarious. If that one with the bottle glassed him, he'd be out of the fight. His Alpha snarled and spat inside him, urging him on, desperate to sink his teeth into fresh violence. He shook his head.

The three men laughed at him, one gobbed at the ground between them, a fat frothing blob of drool.

Noah took another step forward, his whole body taut and straining with contained rage. The men flinched but held their ground, and the line of people around them drew back silently. He jutted his jaw at them with a disdainful smirk, then turned slowly, the line of people parting as he strode through. Behind him the men cat whistled and mocked him, but he kept his chin high and stepped off the pavement onto the road.

Halfway across the road he heard it, a whistling sound. Instinctively he ducked to the side as a bottle came zooming past his ear and smashed on the ground beside him, sticky liquid and shards of glass striking up into the air, smashing against his leg. He winced, then turned — his Alpha now in full control. Snarling, his tight fists almost painful, he pushed his way through the line.

"You fucking pricks!" he screamed. "Where the fuck are you?" But they'd gone. Disappeared. He scanned the line, forcing his way through. One girl whimpered and clung to her friend. Others began to scatter and he could hear whispers of Alpha and dangerous and crazy. It only added to his fury. "Come back, you dickheads!"

He needed to unleash the rage crashing through his body, banging in his head. He needed to hit something, to have his fist connect with flesh and bone. He needed to rip apart anyone who dared to challenge him. Swinging his gaze around, he searched for a target, any target, his rational brain trying to break through, to calm the wolf inside. It dragged him, stumbling with adrenaline, to an alleyway, away from the people and the noise, into the darkness, where the stench of piss and vomit and day-old bin bags pulled him back further to himself.

He leant against the wall, panting, blowing away the anger. His fingers gripped at the brickwork, and then he allowed himself one indulgence. He drew back his left hand, his dominant one, and hit the wall, allowing the pain of his knuckles crunching to wipe everything else clean.

Cora reaches over and takes his hand in hers, pulling it towards her and examining the bruising and scabbing. Her hands are warm against his colder ones, and the brush of her fingers over his knuckles is tender. He has a sudden urge to grasp her hand and sit with her holding hands like two thirteen-year-olds on a date.

He snatches his arm away and removes it from sight under the table.

"That doesn't look like nothing." She's frowning, that crease between her eyebrows defiant. Behind them he can hear the clink of glasses as the barman continues to replace them on the shelf and a slot machine chirps brightly from a corner, attempting to entice a patron. "That looks like a fight!"

"That was me *avoiding* a fight."

She raises an eyebrow. "Right!"

He slumps in his chair and folds his arms across his chest, which brings his injured hand into view. Her gaze travels back there and realising his mistake, he tucks it under his arm, wincing a little.

She glances away, picking up her glass and swilling the amber liquid around in circles. From the corner, the slot machine buzzes with excitement, and the elderly man with the paper scrapes his stall along the floorboards.

Noah doesn't like these silences between them. He likes when they talk, when she bathes him in the sunshine of her attention. He likes to make her smile and occasionally blush. In contrast, the coldness is bone chilling.

Eventually she seems unable to hold in her frustration. "You're going to end up getting kicked out of uni." She shifts forward a little on the bench. Her feet are on the ground now. "Or worse, you could hurt someone — shit — you could get hurt."

"I don't go looking for fights, you know," he snaps.

"Well, they seem to come looking for you."

"Yes, they do!" He lays his injured hand flat on the table, splaying his fingers out wide. His coach hasn't seen his hand yet. He's going to get a bollocking and he'll probably be put on the bench for Saturday's match and made to do extra chores. He flicks his hair away from his face. "You don't understand what it means to be an Alpha."

"Because being an Alpha is so hard! You poor thing."

"You have no idea."

That same rage he sees sparking in her eyes on occasion is there now, flickering, catching alight. She leans forward. "Oh, but I do."

"How?"

She hesitates, as if caught between wanting to win the argument and not wanting to disclose information about herself. There's very little he knows about her, really. In the time they've spent together, she rarely talks about her past or the intimate details of her life. He's placed his tongue inside her cunt, released his come into her mouth, lapped up her slick, and yet he doesn't know where she lived before Oxford or why she has nowhere to go in the holidays. He doesn't even know when her birthday is.

"I've been at the receiving end of Alpha aggression, okay?" She says it quietly to the table, her eyes fixed on his hand.

The room silences. He stills. A chill dances across his skin. The world swoops in merging colours across his vision. His tongue, fat in his mouth, seems to choke him.

Slowly, his words slurred with the warping of time, he says, "What happened?"

She says nothing, and he senses her regret at

having spoken.

"Omega!" His voice is firm despite the quaking of his soul. "Tell me."

Her pupils swim wide and dart up to meet his, responding to the command. She shakes her head slightly, stiffly.

But he won't let it go. He will wrench it from her, if he has to. "Tell me what happened, Omega!"

"It's not what you think, there's no need to get all Alpha about it."

"You just told me—"

"Yes, I know." She looks away towards the bar and then to the door. The air in the pub is warm and yeasty from the ale. A tap hisses from the rear of the pub and a light on the far wall blinks periodically. "It was a long time ago. When I was small."

"Who was it?"

She scrapes her thumb nail down the table like a person clinging on. She opens her mouth to speak. She stops. He waits. Every fiber of his being alert. She swallows. "My father."

His face is neutral. "Right. That's why you don't go home."

"I haven't lived with them for a very long time." A white scratch appears on the table top underneath her nail. "He used to take his aggression out on my mother, sometimes me."

"They removed you."

She nods. "My mother is your typical submissive Omega. His word, his rule, is everything. She's still with him as far as I know."

He stares at her. Bile sloshes in his stomach, burning his throat. It's like finally a light has been switched on; the glaring brightness making everything clear.

"I'm sorry," he mutters, not sure what else to say. He's torn between two primal urges: to gather her up in his arms and soothe away those dark memories, or to hunt down her bastard father and pulverise him into the dirt.

She sighs. "Don't worry about it. It was a long time ago."

"I'd never hurt you," he whispers.

The bench groans as she shifts in her seat. She rubs her eye, grimacing. "It's not... I don't...." Then she looks up at him. "I'm not my mother, not some weak, pathetic girl. I never will be."

"I know." His heart thumps with the need to say more. He struggles. Should he? Things seem so fragile between them; their every encounter laced with trip wires. "It's what I find attractive about you."

"Attractive?" She quirks her head.

"Yes. Attractive."

"You think I'm attractive?"

"It's a cliche that Alphas want some diminutive, submissive Omega. I don't want that." A smile flickers across his face. "I guess I enjoy a woman yelling in my face. You know I find you as hot as hell."

"Yes, I suppose I'd figured it out. From your scent, I mean." She smiles back at him.

And he chuckles. "Shit! Is it that obvious?"

"Only to me."

"Where does that leave us then?"

She reaches over and traces her fingertips around the outline of his hand. "I'm not sure, but I want to take things slowly."

He daren't move, daren't breathe, terrified he'll break the moment.

"I'd like that."

They hold hands as they walk towards the college together, only breaking apart as they get closer. It's so pedestrian after all they've done, yet, of everything, also the most intimate.

Now they are more than friends.

CHAPTER TEN

Noah: I'm watching it
Cora: Errr watching what?
Noah: When Harry met Sally.
Cora: Really?
Noah: Yeah I thought I'd better check it out seeing as it's your favourite movie
Cora: Are you studying me?
Noah: yeah maybe I am.
Cora: Not sure whether I should be flattered or creeped out?
Noah: Flattered.
Cora: But you would say that.
Noah: I like it so far.
Cora: Where are you up to?
Noah: They're watching movies together in bed. In their own beds. It's why I thought to message you.
Cora: Hang on — pause it — let me watch it with you
Noah: What were you doing?
Cora: Watching cat videos and eating chocolate.
Noah: Are you serious?

Cora: Yes. I got my period and I feel like crap.

Noah: Do you want me to get you anything?

Cora: No, I've got my hot toddy. I'll be fine by tomorrow. Right I got it — let's watch? It's so cute right?

Noah: Hmmm

Cora: Okay. I'm calling you. I need to see your face.

"Hi," she says, as the dark screen of her phone gives way to his image. "Oh." He's sat on what must be his bed, shirtless, his bare chest illuminated blue by the light of his laptop. "Do you always video call girls topless?"

"You called me." He smirks. "And it's nothing you haven't seen before."

It's true, and he is beautiful, the contours of his body carefully crafted, but she still finds herself embarrassed, like she's interrupted something intimate. He seems to read her discomfort through the distance of their screens.

"Hang on then." He reaches down off the side of the bed and she gets a view of the muscles in his back rippling as he stretches away, then sits up, pulling a blue t-shirt over his head. "Better?"

She nods, suddenly conscious of the fact she is wearing an old t-shirt and pyjama shorts, with her hair scraped up into a pony and no makeup. She must look like shit.

He settles against the pillows. "I was thinking

about the scene in the cafe, you know the famous one."

"Yeah."

"You've never done that? Faked it when you've been with me."

She laughs. "I've been in heat every time, out of my mind. I don't think I'd be capable of faking anything."

"That's what I thought, but it got me wondering." He folds his arms lazily across his chest and watches for a moment. "You ever faked it with anyone else?"

"Is that a sly way of asking about my previous relationships?"

His eyes flit to meet hers on the screen. "Yeah. I'm trying to work you out."

"You are?"

He nods. "All the time."

"I'm honestly not that complicated." She untwists the elastic from her hair and lets it fall about her shoulders.

"Yes, you are, everybody is."

"Most people are very simple," she says, combing her fingers through her loose hair.

His eyes follow the progress of her hand. "Not to me."

She chews the inside of her cheek, mulling this over. "Sometimes I faked it, not very often, but there were occasions when I did with my last boyfriend."

"Why?"

"It was easier. Like if I wanted him to get on with things or, I suppose, to save his feelings."

"Who was he?" His tone is a tad strained, jealous even.

"No one you know."

Noah shuffles on the bed and switches the phone to the other side. "Was he an Alpha?"

"No, a Beta."

"Ahhh," he says

"Ahh what?"

"I'm not surprised he couldn't make you come."

She rolls her eyes. "Because Alphas are such sex gods."

"No, because sex between an Alpha and Omega is just that way. All the hormones, and phero-mones. It's always intense."

She looks away from him, towards Harry monologuing something cynical on her laptop screen. "I've never been with an Alpha outside a heat." She bites harder on the inside of her cheek. "Actually, you're the only Alpha I've slept with. I've kinda avoided Alphas."

She can almost sense his hot stare on her, but she can't bring herself to turn and meet his gaze.

"Right," he says softly.

Still staring at the screen, she says, "How many Omegas have you been with?"

"A few."

"A few?" Now she looks at him and can tell he doesn't want to answer the question. "How many are a few?"

"None of them were serious. Some flings here, one or two arrangements like we had. Couple of one-night stands."

"Oh."

"I've never dated an Omega before." He holds her gaze.

"Honestly?" She swallows.

"Yes."

The blood seems to swim in her head and her skin burns hot. It's a pleasant sensation, even if there's a sense of panic stirring too.

"You look cute," he says, "when you're thinking."

She furrows her brow. Outside of sex, he's never complemented her like that before. His eyes return to the movie and he leans further into the pillow, sliding his hand under his t-shirt and rubbing his left pec absentmindedly. The plane of his chest and his stomach are somewhere she'd like to lay her head, to snuggle up with his arm around her, engrossed in his scent.

She doesn't watch the rest of the movie; she keeps floating back to him, to observe his micro expressions, to see the movement of his shoulders as he breathes steadily. Occasionally, he glances to his phone and meets her eye, and each time the tension grows fiercer.

"I'm not sure you're watching this movie," he says, when he peers at his phone a fifth time.

"No, I'm not." She hesitates and closes her laptop lid, curling up on her side. "I quite like watching you."

"Come round then and see the real thing." He's pinning her down with the intensity of his eyes.

She shakes her head. "I was serious about taking things slowly. I don't want anyone knowing about us. Not yet." The truth is, she's not sure she'd ever want anyone knowing about this. They'd only jump to their conclusions, judge her, file her away as Noah's Omega. She would be tainted with the same brush as him. All the respect and all the visibility she's built here would vanish into thin air. Poof. Gone. She couldn't go back to that. To not owning a voice, to not being seen or heard.

No, she'd rather have her cake and eat it. And by cake, she means him. No doubt she wants him very much. The urge to touch herself too strong as he stares at her through their screens.

"I wish I could smell you, know what you're thinking little Omega." He stretches out his arm and picks up a tumbler of water, taking two large gulps. He replaces the glass and adds, "although you aren't easy to read. You know how with some Alphas and Omegas their scents are so transparent. Like they've tattooed their emotions on their head. You can read them a mile away, even a little shift in their scent, and it's clear. You're not like that."

"What am I like?"

He chuckles, rubs at his chest again. "Contradictory."

"My scent is contradictory?"

"Yes, not always. When you're in heat, it's pretty overwhelmingly clear what you want."

"Hmmm."

"But even then, there are times when there are so many other emotions mixed in there too and I can't get a hold on it. It's... frustrating."

She nods. Her emotions are such a tangle of contradictions when he's around that she can't even read them herself.

"How about me?" he asks.

"Oh, I'm a hopeless Omega, surely you've realised that by now. I'm no good at reading people's scents."

"I don't believe you. It's intuition. It's a sense all Alphas and Omegas have."

This annoys her. "Well, yes, some of it I read automatically without even engaging my mind. But other times, I can't or I don't trust it." That's the truth of it. "I don't trust Alphas."

"We aren't all bad."

"It doesn't seem that way when you're an Omega. When you consider all the centuries of Alphas using and oppressing Omegas." She hesitates. "When you've seen things first hand."

He nods. "Things have changed."

"Have they? Then why do you Alphas sing those songs when you're wasted, why do so many Omegas end up trapped in relationships they can't leave, why do I lose out on pay whenever I have a heat." She's tired. These abuses are exhausting. Noah, there on the other side, listening to her intently, is simply beautiful. Why can't it be simple? Why can't it just be them? Without all the history and complications. "I'm sorry. I'm tired and grumpy."

"I understand what you're saying."

She waits for the buts, for the excuses, for him to dismiss her worries and angers. He doesn't.

"This film is actually good, " he says. "Although Harry is a knob. Sally is clearly way out of his league."

"Most men are, knobs, I mean." She says it with a smile.

"Yeah, unfortunately sometimes our knobs do the thinking for us."

"Ain't that the truth!" She yawns. "I'm going to go to sleep now. This was fun."

"This was strange, but I liked it. Goodnight, Cora."

"Maybe we can watch another movie another time."

"Yeah... or just chat like this."

She grins. "Goodnight, Noah."

The next week, he comes to the cafe mid-afternoon when she's working and sets up his laptop on a table by the window. He orders an espresso from her and a granola bar stacked with nuts and fruits. From behind the counter, she watches him throw back the contents of his cup and quickly become engaged in his computer, leaving his snack untouched.

The cafe becomes busier as the afternoon passes, the students and workers filing in to grab some caffeine or a sandwich on their way home from work. There's only Cora and Susan working and they are both rushed off their feet, Susan manning the till and Cora the coffee machine. Occasionally, she glances Noah's way as she turns around to hand over an order and once or twice she catches a whiff of him over the tangy smell of coffee and the creamy steam of milk blasting into her face as she heats metal jugs of the stuff.

At six, Susan twists the sign on the door to 'closed' and heads off to leave Cora to lock up. There's only Noah and another table of school girls left in the shop. Cora grabs a damp cloth and heads over to the girls, collecting up their cups and wiping down the table surface. They get the hint, collect up their belongings and leave.

It's late March. The piercing cold of winter morphed to the cool damp air of Spring. Outside, the sun sets behind the tall university buildings and the sky, light at the horizon, darkens to a deep blue, the street lights flickering on. The daffodils that spring from grassy patches around the pavements close their bright yellow heads, ready for the night.

Cora takes the seat next to Noah, their images reflected in the dark window.

"I'm closing up," she says.

He looks up, startled. "Wh-what?"

"It's gone six. I'm closing the cafe."

"Six, shit. I'm never going to get this finished and I've got practice in an hour." He drags his palm over his face.

"What you working on?"

He wrinkles his brow, confused. "This week's essay. What else would I be working on?"

"Video games." She scrubs at a dried crust of cream stuck to the table. "I didn't really take you for the essay type."

He rubs his eye with the heel of his hand, still looking confused. "Doing essays isn't actually optional though, is it?"

She doesn't want to confess to her belief that he'd paid others to write his assignments, so she changes the subject. "I'm going to lock the cash in the safe. Five minutes, okay?"

Shutting the laptop lid, he grabs the hand she's still swiping across the table top and draws her to her feet, gently leading her towards him. Leaning into his chair, his hands resting on her hips, he waits. There's a tension in the air. That line between them pulled tight, like a rubber band about to snap. His scent peaks, a high-pitched roar in her ears.

They've been dancing around this, linked together, stretching the line one moment, allowing it to contract them closer together the next. But it's got shorter and shorter, tauter and tauter, and now it's reeling her in. She lowers her head and meets his waiting lips.

The kiss is so different from anything before. Slow, considered, patient. He caresses first her top lip between his and then her bottom; light, fleeting, tender presses; savouring her as if she were a dish he's longed to taste. She buries her hands into the soft hair at his neck, letting the strands run like water over her fingers, and steps nearer.

The kiss deepens. They slide their tongues into each other's mouths, along the seams of their lips, over the ridges of their teeth. His canines are sharp and she imagines him sinking them into the skin of her gland. She shudders and her scent spirals into the air. He pulls away, his dark pupils wide and alert.

"I have to go, Omega."

She shudders a second time, that word on his lips stupefying every nerve in her body. "Oh," she mutters, unable to keep the disappointment from her voice.

Leaning in, he kisses her stomach and reaches up to smooth his fingers over her aching gland.

"I've got practice. I'm already in the shithouse about my hand. If I'm late...."

She nods, although inside she's wobbling, her frail Omega distressed that he's leaving.

Later, when she tries to unpick the strange reaction, it frightens her. It reminds her of that dependency she'd once experienced. The way another Alpha had drawn her in.

She'd been 15, alone, and vulnerable; completely naïve to the new world she'd entered. The Alpha had been older, good looking and charming. He'd said she was special, that he loved her, that he'd take care of her. He made her feel all those things: special, loved, cared for. But there were other feelings too: controlled, trapped, frightened. He had opinions on what she should wear, how she should behave and where she should go, and he'd been angry with her when she'd confessed she wasn't ready to sleep with him.

No matter how many times he'd told her he loved her, the accompanying feeling of suffocation didn't seem right. In the end she'd needed to tell someone and had skipped school to find Jaz, a social worker only a few years older than she was and an Omega herself. Cora had hoped that someone like that could help her understand. Was this how it felt to be an Omega?

If Jaz had been surprised or concerned to see her there in the middle of the day, dressed in her navy school skirt, white blouse and striped tie, she hadn't shown it. Calmly she'd led her to a meeting room that the council had tried to deck out in a way that made it seem homely with a small sofa and two armchairs.

Cora had curled herself up in the chair and tried to explain the situation. It had been hard at first to find the words. She'd always known she was different, that something was wrong with her, and these emotions seemed to confirm it. Shouldn't she be pleased to have found an Alpha? To have found someone who finally cared about her?

Gradually Jaz had coaxed it all out of her, quietly asking her questions and prompting her.

"Does this seem normal to you, Cora?" Jaz had asked, and she'd shaken her head. "How do you think love should feel?"

She'd considered that for a long time because truly she wasn't sure. "Safe?"

"Yes. I think you are correct. You should feel safe with the one you love. Anything else?"

"I don't know."

Jaz had twisted the chunky silver ring she wore on her right middle finger and swallowed. "I've been in love a couple of times, Cora. Unfortunately, it didn't work out for various reasons. But when I was in love, it felt... freeing. It wasn't confusing. At the time it just felt right." She'd examined Cora's face. "You're a smart kid, Cora. I wonder if you already know the answer to all this."

Cora nodded. "It doesn't feel right. But does that mean there's something wrong with me?"

"No, Cora, absolutely not." Jaz had taken a long breath out and told her then, "This Alpha is known to us. Do you understand what I'm saying? He is known as an Alpha who grooms young Omegas."

Jaz had shipped her away to another home and another town after that and a couple of years later Cora had learned that the Alpha had landed in prison.

Is this the same? she thinks. Noah Wood is not a nice person. The grazes on his knuckles are proof of that.

CHAPTER ELEVEN

It's Rose's birthday, and she wants to go out dancing, to blow off steam and forget about the upcoming final exams and the increasing mess that is her family. It's something Cora hasn't done in a while — she hasn't had the money — but Rose is so keen, she can't say no.

Perhaps a night out, drinking and dancing, some time to forget about all the confusion in her heart and in her mind is what she needs. Her growing relationship with Noah, this secret, has been an uneasy burden weighing down on her shoulders.

Rose knocks on Cora's bedroom door.

"Which one?" she asks, holding up a red and a black dress.

"Hmmmm. I think if you wanna make an impression, the black."

"I was thinking of wearing it with my colourful necklace — the beaded one."

"Oh yeah — that'll look nice."

"Hair up or down?"

"Definitely down." Rose has beautiful thick shiny hair and Cora can't understand why she'd ever choose to wear it up.

"Fab," Rose pauses, 'what are you wearing — you are coming, aren't you?"

"Yeah, yeah, it's your birthday, of course I'm coming," she says, shutting her laptop lid. "But I'm not sure what to wear — urgh, I don't have anything."

"How about my backless top with your skinny trousers?"

"Really?"

"Yeah, Cora — you'd look awesome in that with your hair scooped up. And you never know there might be some cute guys there tonight. Joe will be there. I'm pretty sure he likes you."

Cora's never been bothered about hooking up with guys — it doesn't tend to go well when you're an Omega. Usually she's fighting off lecherous Alphas who think they just have to click their fingers and she'll go trotting off after them.

On the occasion she meets a nice Beta they either get freaked out when they realise she's an Omega or they think she'll be up for some dubious shit. Besides, there's this thing with Noah. They've not defined it yet, and they've not made any promises to each other. But undeniably something is happening between them.

Not that she can tell Rose any of this. She won't understand.

Rose spins around. "Can I grab the first shower?"

"Sure."

Later, Cora twists in front of the mirror, wondering if she looks okay. It's strange having her back bare and her gland exposed. It makes her vulnerable. She runs her fingers over the gland, recalling a certain pair of lips skirting over her paper thin skin there.

"Cora! You ready?" Rose calls from the hallway and Cora grabs her purse and jacket and skips out. "Woah, you look amazing, lady. You're gonna have every guy in there hitting on you."

Cora rolls her eyes. She really doesn't want that — there's only one man's attention she wants. "Thank you — you look beautiful too."

The doorman looks them up and down with an appreciative eye and runs his finger over the list, letting them pass when he finds Rose's name. It's already late, and the place is crowded; the air thick with perfume and alcohol. They push their way through the hot bodies, Cora's hand in Rose's, until they reach the table. Their friend Zach is already there with a handful of others, and he leaps to his feet and wraps Rose in a hug.

"It's the birthday girl! Wow, you girls are stunning." He pulls Rose down onto an empty stool and Cora finds a space on the bench seat. "We already got a couple of jugs of cocktail," he points to the stack of glasses, "drink up!"

Cora takes the glass offered and whips down the drink, the liquid cool in her throat. It's then that she catches a whiff of Noah, the hairs on her arms rising at that hint of him here, her body automatically reacting to his unseen presence.

Noah. Here.

And Rose too. And all her friends. It's too complicated. Hopefully he'll stay out of her way.

She can't hear the conversation between Zach and Rose, the deep beat of the music too powerful, and so she pours herself another drink, knocking that one down quickly too, the alcohol hitting her bloodstream and giving her a pleasant buzz.

She rolls her head from side to side, trying to ignore the unease that lingers somewhere in her mind and hone in on that buzz instead. She takes another drink and leans over the table.

"Can we dance?" she whines.

Rose throws up her hands in protest. "I'm not wasted enough yet."

"I am," says Zach, jumping to his feet and flinging out his hand. "May I have this dance, Madam?" he adds, with a flamboyant bow.

Cora holds her hand to her chest and flutters her eyelashes. "Why, I'd be delighted!"

Zach tugs her to her feet and twirls her under his arm. "Follow me then, " he says, pulling her after him as he saunters through the club, hips wiggling, his spare hand waving above his head in time to the music. When he reaches the dancefloor, he spins Cora into him and spirals them around. She flings back her head laughing, her concerns flying away, the other people dizzy faces under the flashing spotlights.

She stumbles and Zach catches her, slinging her backwards against his arm, and then swishing her onto her feet. Grabbing his shoulder, she leans into him, giggling wildly, until she senses Noah. Without seeing him, she knows he's nearby, hovering in the dark spaces at the edge of the dance-floor. She can almost sense his gaze on her and her skin burns, the Omega inside her skittish and on edge.

It's not like she's doing anything wrong. Only having a bit of fun. Only dancing with her friend. Yet there's something in his scent that frightens her. Something angry and possessive.

"Can we go sit down for a bit?" she yells into Zach's ear, and his fingertips rest on her waist, pulling her closer so he can hear as she does. Noah's anger spikes invisibly in the air and she forces herself not to jump.

It pisses her off. He doesn't own her. She's not his. She is free to do what she wants, and, God, if she won't fight tooth and nail to always retain that freedom.

She pulls Zach away towards the recesses of the bar, wanting to be hidden. But no sooner do they stop, than Noah is there, towering above them.

Zach looks up at him in confusion, and Noah glares at him. He flicks his eyes to Cora.

"You want to dance?" he growls.

She twists away from him. "No." Her anger is as clear as his own, peaking above the stench of sweaty bodies and sticky alcohol.

"Omega," he barks and Zach's eyes widen, his gaze swinging to Cora and then Noah.

"I don't want to."

"Then let's talk."

"She said no." Zach puffs out his chest, attempting to position himself between her and Noah.

The Alpha's scent grows dangerous, and she's suddenly frightened — for Zach more than herself.

"Fine," she says to Noah, a warning shot in her eyes, and turns to Zach. "Sorry, I'll be right back."

"Cora?" Zach says with uncertainty.

She squeezes his hand. "It's fine. Will you get us some more drinks?"

It's clear he doesn't want to leave her, but she squeezes his hand tighter and gives him a nod.

When he's gone, she spins to Noah, folding her arms across her body.

"What was that?"

"What!?! I only asked you to dance."

"Bullshit. That was you pissing all over me and marking me up as your territory."

"And what do you expect me to do, stand back and watch some other guy letch all over you?"

"He wasn't. Zach is my friend. My very gay friend." She grits her teeth. "I'm not interested in Alpha bullshit, Noah."

"Well, what exactly are you interested in then? Because sorry if I got the impression you were interested in me."

It hits her hard in the middle of her ribs. Yes she is, she is interested in him. She wants him. And yet she knows there are people watching all around; judging and condemning her.

"I told you. I want to take it slow." She digs her fingers into the flesh of her arms, trying to regain some control in her head. "I'm not ready for people to know."

He snaps his head, tossing the hair from his face, and holds his hands out.

"Don't you think every Omega and Alpha already knows about us?"

"How?! You told them."

"No." He scowls in annoyance. "They can smell it. It's fucking obvious."

What? *What?* The possibility had never occurred to her, and yet it's so damn obvious. What a fool she is!

"Why haven't they said anything?"

"They're being discreet. They know we haven't gone public. They know what it means to do that, all the gossip, all the pressure. There's an unwritten code between Omegas and Alphas: don't talk about other people's relationships. We get enough shit as it is without our own people adding to it."

She feels lightheaded. There's a code? Nobody has ever taught her about these things. She's that lost teenager all over again, trying to make her way in a complicated world she doesn't understand. In a quiet voice she asks, "Do the Betas know?"

"I doubt it. You'd know if they did."

There's bile rising in her throat; her hands

shake.

"Cora," he says, the animosity gone from his tone.

But then Rose is there, agitated, aggressive.

"What's going on?" she demands, positioning herself between Cora and Noah. "Is he hassling you?"

Cora goes to answer, but she doesn't get the chance.

"Just because you're an Alpha doesn't give you the right to hit on her." Rose takes Cora's hand possessively in hers.

Noah shakes his head at her, sneering with feigned amusement. "Go away, will you; this is none of your business."

"Fuck if it isn't," Rose says, stabbing a finger towards him. "This is my best friend. And this isn't the 18th century. You don't get to command Omegas anymore." Rose's voice rises, she's winding up for a full on lecture, Cora can sense it. She tries to tug her away, but Rose remains feet planted, her grip on Cora tightening. "Did you know he's been spreading rumours about the two of you?"

"What?" Cora whispers. Noah looks as shocked as she feels.

"Yep, been going around bragging that he's sleeping with you."

"No, I haven't," he growls, his scent spiking. She waits for him to say more, to inform her friend the rumours are true. But he remains silent.

"You're scum. You know that." Rose continues.

"They should've thrown you out after the first term. The only reason you're still here is your family and your wealth. You make me sick."

Zach joins them, a glass tumbler in each hand, his face drained with alarm. "Is everything alright?"

"No, he's harassing Cora."

Cora can see Noah's struggling. Rose is like a kid with a stick poking the bear, with every fresh jab, his irritation growing. His nostrils flare as he sucks in each breath and his hands are balling and stretching.

He paces forward. "You have no fucking idea. Piss off! I was talking to Cora, not you."

Rose steps forward too. "You were intimidating her."

"Rose!" Cora cries, but she's too late, everything blows up and despite her attempt she can't smother the spark on the fuse.

As Rose yanks forward, Cora pulls on her hand and Zach jumps between Rose and Noah, just as Noah attempts to reach towards her. There's a clash of arms and shoulders and torsos, a glass flies into the air, Rose yells, Noah pushes the bodies away, and Zach flies backwards, slamming into the wall, tumbling to the ground, his hand sliced by the broken glass around him as he tries to steady himself.

Cora dashes towards him, crouching down by his side.

There's blood. Lots of blood. Rose is screaming

at Noah now, pummelling his chest with her fists. People push past them. Someone yells for an ambulance. Another for the police. There're words jumbling in the crowd around them. Assault. Attack. Alpha.

Noah stands motionless in the centre as people rush about him, trying to reach Zach slumped behind him, his head nodding as blood flows from his arm.

She meets Noah's eyes, wide with fear and alarm.

"It was an accident," he says to her, the words clear above the shouting and the deep boom of the base. "I didn't mean to do it."

She can hear others around them, bouncers pushing through the people.

"Go home, Noah," she shouts at him, her heart hammering so loudly in her skull she hardly hears her own words, her vision swimming with Zach's crimson blood. "Go home."

Noah's hands shake as he forces his way through the crowd, knocking away the arms that try to grab him, ignoring commands for him to stop.

She takes Zach's injured hand in her own, blood rushing onto her fingers and her palms. The cut is bad, deep and long. She yells for some help and somebody shoves a wad of paper napkins at her, Holding his hand in one of hers, she uses her free hand and her teeth to unwind the serviettes and then wrap them tightly around his injury, attempting to pull the ripped skin back together, and raising his arm above his head.

A bouncer kneels down and hooks Zach's good arm around his neck, leading him away, while another sweeps away the glass and two more push away the gathered gawkers. Rose rushes towards Cora, flinging her arms around her neck.

"Oh god, Cora! Are you okay?"

"Yes," she stutters, "yes I'm fine."

But she's not fine. She's anything but as she races after Zach.

CHAPTER TWELVE

Cora doesn't like hospitals. She doesn't like the stark strip-white lighting or the strong acid and metallic smells. She doesn't like the fierce ripping sound the curtains make when people drag them around cubicles or the hard touch of the straight-backed chairs. She doesn't like the scent of fear, pain and death that hang in every molecule of the air or the concern etched on grey, tired faces.

The shock that had grasped Zach as they'd raced across town in a taxi has faded and he is back to his loud and cheerful self, talking animatedly to the skinny male nurse who is cleaning his wound.

Cora tries to focus in on their good-humoured banter, smiling when Zach makes a joke and nodding when he turns to her for confirmation, but it's difficult when this place feels like a time warp, as if it's sucking her back to places she doesn't want to go.

A hard-backed chair; only it was larger then,

almost swallowing up her tiny frame. The same scents, the same faces plus hushed voices, people swirling around the bed, her mother laid out motionless, her face almost unrecognisable through the swollen flesh.

It's how she had found her. After the shouting stopped and the front door slammed, she had crept down the stairs and found her mother lying on the cold kitchen floor. For a long moment, an endless moment, that was the very worst of her short, little life, she'd thought her mother was dead, but then her mother's head had snapped towards her, battered and sore, and murmured her name.

She'd known what to do (it wasn't the first time she'd needed to find a phone and dial 999), and then she'd curled up against her mum, taking her big hand in her own and listened to the rasps of her breath.

The two paramedics had argued with the police officers in hushed tones about what to do with her. In the end, she'd been allowed to sit in the front of the ambulance and press the button to turn on the siren and the blue flashing lights. At the hospital an elderly nurse, round like a pudding, had checked her over and read her a story about a friendly tiger. But she'd gone and they had left Cora to wait alone in the hard, cold chair.

"All done," says the nurse to Zach, tying the ends of the bandage together. "If it's giving you any pain, you can take some ibuprofen. It will help with any swelling too. Take the bandage off in a day or two and keep the wound cleaned but dry. Any strange smells or pus or sudden temperatures, go see your GP."

"Thanks mate," says Zach, holding his bandaged hand out towards Cora. "I look like a Zombie."

"You smell like one too." Cora grins.

They catch a taxi into town and silently they watch darkened houses and empty streets flash past the window, listening to the drone of some talk show host on the car's radio. Cora rests her head on Zach's shoulder and threads her arm through his uninjured one.

"I'm sorry," she says.

"For what? It wasn't your fault."

The next day Cora rises late to find her WhatsApp chat has been streaming nonstop with discussions about what happened the night before. What starts as a tale of a bit of a push in a bar evolves into a full out unprovoked assault, and Zach's brief trip to the hospital to have his cut glued together becomes a dash in an ambulance, an emergency operation to save his hand and the need for a blood transfusion.

Sitting at her desk, trying to read the books she needs to finish before she can start her essay, she's continually distracted by the vibration of her phone. The buzz starting as a slow rhythm and becoming faster and more frantic, her mobile skimming across her desk; the screen flickering with message after message.

She opens her drawer and shoves the device inside where it continues to chirp incessantly. She reads a line. Stops. Realises she took nothing in. Then reads again. The phone is too tempting. Her fingers keep flicking to the drawer before she stops herself.

It's better not to know. It will all blow over soon enough. Surely.

She wants to put things right, to explain what really happened, but the story has already run away from her in the hours she'd been at the hospital and sleeping. She can't catch it back. By the end of the day it's on Twitter and there are photos on Instagram. People are calling for Noah's head. There are long rants about Alpha aggression and privilege, the vitriol growing angrier and angrier. The few voices that try to intervene, to offer a different perspective, are engulfed in flames of abusive fire and swiftly retreat. She's frightened to get involved, to expose herself.

Soon the old stories about him are pulled out. The rumours swirl and swell, gathering such pace she's left breathless. She hardly recognises the man they describe; he's a demon, a monster, a maniac. Not her Noah at all.

Noah himself is silent. Just one message sent in the minutes after the event.

It was an accident.

That's all. She was at the hospital and had never replied, and as the minutes turn to hours turn to days, her own anger gives way to guilt.

Yes she'd been furious. How could he let that happen? How could he do that? Why couldn't he just walk away? Yes, Rose had been in his face, downright rude and insulting, but he could've turned away. Instead, he let his anger get the better of him once again. She was so disappointed in him. And scared — it was all too familiar.

But now there's this guilt. He's right. It was an accident. She knows that. And she never returned his message. Never checked he was alright, didn't defend him, hasn't tried to clear up this mess. Those aren't the actions of someone who is meant to care about you.

He must hate her. He should. She hates herself. Despises her own weakness, and her cold heart. She is ashamed of herself.

Rose doesn't seem to notice Cora's despondency. She's right in the thick of it all, loving the chance to launch an attack at the Alpha community and its poster boy.

Four days after the event, Rose is still riding the wave of outrage.

"We're launching a petition," she tells Cora as she pours muesli into a white bowl, shaking the packet violently so that the flakes fall out in clumps. "Demanding the university investigate — you know the police aren't interested despite it being assault. I bet his mother knows someone in the department or something. So it's up to the university to take action."

Cora lowers her piece of toast. "Rose! That's —"

"I know you're intimidated, but you've been really quiet on Twitter. You've got to be vocal, Cora. Otherwise these Alphas will continue to get away with this bullshit."

Cora knows this is nothing to do with Noah or Alphas. It's her dad Rose is angry at and she's finding something to take that anger out on. It had been the week before that they had sat at this table, eating ice cream together, when Rose's phone had beeped with a message. She'd paused halfway through her story to read it, her eyes flicking across the screen and then the smile on her face slipping and her skin turned white.

"What? What is it, Rose?" Cora had asked, unease in her stomach.

"It's my Dad."

"Your dad? Is he okay?"

"He's fine... he's having a baby. I mean, Melanie's having a baby."

"She's pregnant?"

"Yes. More than six months pregnant, apparently. And he's only telling me now. By text. By *text*." She'd laughed bitterly. "He's 54. He'll be 75 by the time the kid is our age." Then tears had slid down her cheeks and she'd buried her face in her hands. "I can't believe he's doing this. I always wanted a brother or sister growing up. I used to beg them all the time for one. My mum wanted more children, you know. It was him who didn't."

Cora had crouched down beside her and rubbed her hand up and down her back.

"My mum is going to be a mess. I need to tell her before she finds out from someone else."

This anger of Rose's has had nowhere to go. Her father is on the other side of the ocean. She can't shout at him. She can't yell at him. Instead, Rose has channeled this fury into this campaign and they've had the same argument every day; Rose trying to rally Cora into action, Cora attempting to make her see reason. It's no use. Rose isn't listening and Cora is tired.

Cora takes her plate to the sink, treading down on the pedal of the bin so that the lid lifts with a snap and sliding her toast into the waiting bag.

"I'm going back to bed."

"What? Don't you have a tutorial this morning?"

Cora shrugs and heads to her bedroom, shutting the door on the concerned enquiries of her friend. She climbs into bed and pulls the covers around herself. There's a temptation to reach for her phone and see what everyone is saying today, but she resists. It'll only add to the sickness in her stomach. She flips onto her back and stares at the ceiling. A thin fissure crack traces from one corner to the next and the bland lampshade hangs at a crooked angle.

She remembers he'd huffed at it once and stood on her bed, naked, and tried to straighten it. When he'd failed, every movement angling it more acutely, she burst into a fit of giggles and he'd pinned her to the bed and blew raspberries on her stomach, their laughter switching to lust as he'd hardened and rubbed against her.

She closes her eyes and flops her arm over her face. The day passes. The shadows shift across the room as the sun loops up into the sky and then down to the horizon. She hears Rose leave, her boots clicking in the hallway, and return much later with a rattle of the front door. At some point, as her room darkens, the aroma of baking potatoes wafts down the hallway and Rose knocks on her door to ask if she wants anything to eat.

"No," she mutters, rolling onto her side, burying her face into the bed. She can almost convince herself that there's still the faintest hint of him lingering in the mattress. If she screws up her eyes and concentrates only on her nose, she can conjure it up, believe it's real. It makes a part of her ache, something inside her tight chest.

Eventually the house is quiet, the noise of traffic outside subsides and blackness engulfs her room, but she doesn't sleep. Her brain refuses to rest, reliving the events in the bar. Noah's solemn face clear in her mind, as if he's judging her.

How did she let this happen? How did she let someone get under her skin like this? It's what she's tried so hard to avoid, determined to never let anyone hurt her again. And yet, deep down she knows it isn't Noah who has hurt her, she's hurt herself.

The night passes in these dark thoughts, her tired head tormented and tortured, and by morning exhaustion finally overwhelms her. When she wakes some hours later, her skin is hot and her neck tingling. Her heat. She'd forgotten all about it. Easter break starts in a week and so does her heat. It's what she deserves; to suffer it alone and miserable.

CHAPTER THIRTEEN

The corridor, lined in chestnut paneling, is dark and empty. An ancient grandfather clock in the corner ticks loudly, two weights swinging from below its face, and behind one of the doors there's a low murmur of voices and the tapping of keys. Old oil paintings of grim looking men hang on the walls, each seeming to stare at Noah with disapproval.

It's stuffy and formal — an attempt, he thinks, to remind those waiting outside on the hard wooden seats of the authority and power of the man who owns the office behind him.

It's not the first time he's sat on one of these chairs awaiting an appointment with the Dean. He's been here before, after the stupid fight that spiralled out of his control at the end of his first term.

That time he'd perched on this same chair with terror, regret and anger. His mother had been with him, whispering terse words of disapproval, and he'd sweated so hard his shirt had stuck to his underarms beneath his jacket.

This time he hasn't brought her. He can't bear more words of reproach. He knows what he is — he needs no reminder from her. And anyway, this time he is numb to it all. Like it's happening to someone else and not to him. Honestly, he couldn't care less what happens to him next. He'll state his side of the facts, but it won't matter, they've all made up their minds about him, anyway.

It's all over social media — he's actually surprised his mother hasn't heard it somehow already — and he's read what they're saying about him. Some of his friends from the rugby team have tried to wade in and back him up, but they were quickly drowned out and attacked themselves. Noah hasn't got involved. He's remained silent. Despite the hate he harbours for himself, he knows it was an accident. He didn't mean for it to happen.

A short grey man, with glasses balanced on the bridge of his nose, takes a step out in the corridor.

"Ah Mr Wood, come in, please."

"Yes, Sir," Noah says, following him inside and standing in front of the large oak desk, while the older man sits down. Behind him are two long windows, and the light throws the Dean into shadow so that Noah has to squint to read his face.

The man keeps Noah waiting, opening a paper file and flicking through some printed pages. Bookcases dominate the room, stuffed with what looks like a combination of ancient leather-bound books and newer, brighter publications. A huge, stone fireplace breaks up the space with another painting hung above, this time a capture of the university from older times, when the surrounding area was greener and more spacious.

Noah remains still, not fidgeting. He feels nothing. Not nerves, not annoyance. There is no hurry.

He wonders if Cora knows that he's here. Kyle is the only person he's told, but his coach will know and his tutors and probably someone spotted him heading into the building. It will be all over the university by now, the latest installment in the story. But has it reached her ears yet?

The end of term is in a week. Usually she'd be timing her heat for the holiday. But he's smelt no hint of it in her scent. Perhaps she's adjusted her suppressants. She won't want to share it with him now. Everything between them is ruined. The moment she told him to go in the club, he'd known. A shifting in the strange connection they share, like the wind suddenly changing direction. A warm southerly breeze giving way to a bitter northerly.

One message is all he's allowed himself to send her. He may be a fool, but he understands when he's not wanted. She hasn't responded and he won't send another. He doesn't need to be told twice.

The numbness in his limbs and in his skull crept in soon after, as if a heavy weight had crushed down on him and cut off the blood supply. It's so severe there isn't even the sensation of pins and needles when he massages his arms, rubs his forehead.

Is it because of her? Or the huge trampling of defeat? The knowledge that he'll always fail no matter how hard he tries — the odds never stacked in his favour and his own faults tripping him up every time.

He stares at the glint of glass behind the man, counting slowly in his head.

Finally, the Dean, removing his glasses, gestures towards the seat in front of his desk.

"Please sit down, Mr Wood," he says.

Noah starts and then pulls out the chair, the legs squeaking against the polished floorboards.

"This is the second time you've been called to my office."

"Yes, Sir."

"Both times with regard to assault."

Noah says nothing. Not knowing whether to dispute the fact or let it lie.

The man sighs. "Every few years we go through the same rigmarole. Some Alpha lets his aggression get the better of him and we have uproar from the students and the faculty — calling for exclusions and segregation and god knows what else. Honestly, you folk don't help yourselves."

Cora wouldn't sit here and take that bullshit. She'd call out the bigotry and prejudice. But he's not Cora and he's so tired of it all. If he argues back, it'll only confirm what the man thinks of him and

Alphas already — always up for a fight.

"A second offence such as this would normally warrant an expulsion." The man places his elbows on the table, leaning a little further forward as if inspecting Noah more closely.

Noah jerks his head in what is barely a nod.

The man continues. "But the other gentleman in question has written to me. He says in his communication that he is aware of lots of false information circulating and wanted to put things straight. He is utterly convinced the incident that caused his injury was an unfortunate accident."

Noah's eyes dart up from his shoes to the Dean.

"He wrote to you to say that?"

"Is he correct, Mr Wood?"

Noah scrubs his hand over his jaw. "I pushed past him — in all honesty, a bit too roughly — I could feel my temper rising and I was trying to leave. I pushed him too hard and he fell, cut himself on some glass."

"I see," the man lowers his glasses to the table. "It seems you owe this man a depth of gratitude."

"I'm kind of stunned," Noah says honestly. "Usually," he shuffles on his seat, looking out towards the blank window, "people want to believe the worst of me — are happy to see me condemned."

"Yes, well," the Dean says, unconvinced. "I am going to have to consider how to handle this — I have a very angry section of the student body, but you have your finals next term and I wouldn't want to deny you your chance in life over what both sides seem to amicably agree was an accident. And Mr Wood, I have to confess that your grades are very good and you have represented the university in Rugby. Your coach speaks highly of you."

Noah nods again. They're going to let him stay. He can't believe it. Shouldn't he feel relieved, happy even?

"So on reflection, I won't be excluding you. I will ask the Proctors to carry out an informal investigation to satisfy the mob. But this will be a formality. The other man's word will see to that."

"Thank you," Noah mumbles.

"You are very fortunate indeed, young man. Accident or not, you seem to find a way of attracting trouble. I strongly advise you to keep your head down and focused on your studies. Get through your finals without any more such trouble. Understood?"

"Yes, sir."

He doesn't check his phone as he leaves the university building, but slides his coat over his suit jacket, pulling up the hood and plugging in his earphones. Shoving his hands in his pocket, he keeps his eyes fixed on the pavement and heads in the direction of home, hoping he won't get accosted by anyone on campus. He doesn't know if anyone would start on him, but he's been keeping a low profile anyway, sticking to the house and to Rugby practice.

The path around the back of the science labs is

always quieter, just a few labs rats smoking hurried cigarettes in their five minute breaks. He hugs the building, tuning into the thud of his music and blocking out the world around him. Half way along the building's length, he turns the sharp corner of the path and walks straight into Cora.

"Oh hi," she says, her face squirming with a mix of emotions. Shock, horror, shame? Her scent spirals in an equally confused concoction, and he swallows.

"Hey." He scuffs at the ground with his shoe and peers over her shoulder, as if he's impatient to leave, like he doesn't want to stop and talk to her, when really there is nothing he'd rather do.

"I'm sorry I didn't see you there."

"No, no. Me neither."

A tight crease forms between her eyebrows, and he recognises it means she's thinking hard. "Are you okay?"

"Yeah, you're pretty small. No damage done."

A hint of a sad smile passes over her face before she frowns again. "Well, good, but I didn't mean that. I meant about, you know." She shrugs and shoves her own hands deep inside her jacket.

"It's..." He struggles to know what to say. "They're not kicking me out, so that's one thing."

"Kick you out?" The colour drains from her face.

"Yeah — I've just been to see the Dean."

"Shit." Her hands twist in her pockets.

"Your friend and her little gang of activists

won't be very happy about it."

"My friend? Rose? She's got nothing to do with this."

His anger flashes. "Yes she has. She's been stirring that group up, the one who's always had a problem with us Alphas." He takes a deep inhale, twisting his head away from her. Then he stills, rubbing his temple. "You're going into heat."

"Yes, next week." A door on the science building opens and a skinny man in a dirty lab coat steps out, already cupping a lighter to his lips. They wait for him to spot them and slink further down the building.

An acidic sickly smell wafts towards them from the closing door, and the burnt singe of tobacco.

They both wait for the other to speak. The weight on his shoulders growing heavier and heavier until he expects his knees to buckle under him. He wants to look at her and show her how much he's hurting, how much it's killed him not to have her to talk to while the world around him has been falling apart. But why would she care?

"Will you come?" she says, her voice catching in her throat.

He screws up his eyes, the pressure in his skull painful. "You want me to?"

"Only if you want to, I mean, you don't have to."

"I'll come." In the distance the smoker kicks at the scrub growing close up against the wall, and there are faint footsteps crunching on the path behind them.

Her scent, so taut and on edge, relaxes, and his shoulders do the same. He peers at her. She's chewing her bottom lip.

How did it get like this? His own stupidity, that's how. Is she giving him a second chance or is this just sex? An Omega in need of an Alpha. This hurt, already so unbearable, will only worsen if he does this, if he sleeps with her again, but when has he ever been able to say no to her.

"I'll see you then," he says, "I've got to go."

CHAPTER
FOURTEEN

Rose hangs about the flat, seeming to take an age to pack her bag. She's spending the Easter break with her mum, who's over from the states visiting the sites around Britain. She was meant to leave this morning, but she's still here at lunchtime.

Cora does her usual pre-heat prep. Waxing, shaving, washing the sheets and pulling out the extra comforter and pillows from the cupboard. Faffing about her room, rearranging stuff. Already she's hot and irritable, wishing Rose would leave and Noah arrive, forcing herself not to glance at her watch every few minutes.

At one o'clock, Rose knocks on her door. "I'm cooking pasta before I leave. You want some?"

"No," Cora snaps, then pulls an apologetic smile. "I'm fine."

"What are you doing in here?" Rose asks, surveying the strange array of pillows on the bed and Cora's neatly arranged belongings.

"A bit of spring cleaning."

"Right — well, maybe you'd like to do the kitchen. When was the last time you cleaned it? I always end up doing it — and the bathroom too."

"Sure," Cora says, wanting her friend to leave.

Noah is due to arrive at one thirty. He'd texted her the night before to confirm the arrangement; short, business-like messages that made her shiver. She picks nervously at the skin around her thumb, dithering about whether to try to sneak him into her room or whether to tell him to come later. She's not sure she can wait though; the pain in her abdomen has her wincing and hunching over. She rubs her nose, a sniffle building in her throat.

She wants him. To hold her. To tell her everything will be alright. For things to be right between them.

It's such a mess. In her head, and in her heart. And the sentimental and fragile Omega inside her is taking over.

The sound of pots banging in the kitchen makes her want to scream. Get out, Rose! Just get out!

How could she think like that about her best friend? She curls up on the bed, dragging the cover over her and tucking it under her arms, shivering despite the burning of her skin.

She closes her eyes, moaning as a violent spasm pulsates in her stomach. She glances at her watch, five minutes. Wrapping the blanket around her, she decides to go wait on the doorstep where she can intercept him before he knocks on the door. On shaking legs she stumbles down the hallway and out of the door, climbing to sit on the low brick wall between their front garden and the neighbour's.

After a few minutes she spots him at the end of the road, dressed in a dark t-shirt and jeans with his usual duffel bag. Her stomach does a little growl as if it's hungry and has sensed food. He's scrolling through his phone as he walks so he doesn't see her until he stops at the pavement outside her house and looks up.

"Hey. You alright?" he says.

She shakes her head, trembling. "Rose is still here."

His shoulders tighten. "Right. What do you want to do?"

"I... I don't know," she mumbles, wanting to breathe in his scent, knowing it will calm her aching body but unsure it's wise.

"I assume she doesn't know I'm coming then."

"No, of course not."

He huffs, his eyebrows twitching. "Wouldn't want her to know you're fucking a violent thug."

"Noah, you know it's not like that."

"I do," he takes a step forward and stares down at her with cold, angry eyes. "I know it's exactly like that." He snorts out through his nose, the whole of his body as taut as his shoulders. "Go distract her, Omega, and I'll come inside."

She nods and shuffles off the wall. Everything hurts, and her movements are laboured. Noah takes her elbow and guides her down. His touch is electric on her skin, and his grip tightens, his fingers sinking into her flesh.

"Fuck, you smell good," he mutters and follows her cautiously into the hallway, hanging back to ensure the coast is clear.

Motioning for him to wait, she shuffles along the hall and into the kitchen, closing the door behind her. Rose sits at the table eating pasta, listening to the politics show on the radio.

"Are you okay, Cora?" She says looking up. "You don't look so well."

"I'm fine. My heat's coming on."

Rose screws up her nose. "Oh sorry, Cora. Can I get you anything?"

"No, I'm sorted, but thanks." She goes to the kettle and flicks it on with her forefinger. "When you off?"

"Hmmmm. Mom's plane got delayed a couple of hours. I pushed back my taxi but it should be here in 30." She twists some tagliatelle around her fork. "Will you be okay? You didn't say you were expecting your heat."

Cora shrugs as the kettle bubbles noisily behind her and steam rises from the spout.

"I'm going to make some tea and hopefully get some sleep. I hope you have a great trip Rose. Don't forget to send me photos, okay?"

Rose smiles. "Sure. Message me if you need to,

right?"

"Yep." A loud click sounds and Cora pours the boiling water onto a waiting tea bag with a hiss. She mashes the bag against the bottom of the China mug until the water stains brown, then scoops it out and tops it up with a dash of cold milk.

Clutching her tea, she hobbles out of the kitchen, stopping to give Rose a little hug.

"Gosh, you're hot."

"Yep."

"Feel better!"

She closes the door behind her again and hurries down the hallway to her room. He's waiting for her on her bed, sitting with his arms stretched out behind him, leaning back, his long legs dangling off the bed and towards the floor. He's in his socks, his trainers positioned in a corner of the room.

Closing her eyes, she swallows up his scent, allowing it to sink into her like sun on skin, the warming effect the same. She takes a sip of the tea. Then offers it to him.

"Want some?" she whispers.

"What is it?" he whispers back, watching her.

"Tea."

He shakes his head. "Is she gone yet?"

"In the next 30 minutes."

"Come here," he says.

"She's only down the hall."

"Come here, Omega."

The name tugs at her centre and her feet carry her towards him without thinking.

"We can be quiet," he growls into her neck as his hands rest on her arse.

"I don't think I can," she sighs as he tugs her onto his lap, sucking hard at her throat.

He covers her mouth with his hand. "You'll be quiet for me, Omega."

She can tell he's in rut. His tone is authoritative, overwhelming. She's his in this moment, to do with as he wants. Gone is his usual caution and concern. He's usually so careful with her, clearly considering every step and each word. But now it's like he can't hold back. He is going to take what he wants.

The thought has slick dampening her underwear and his nostrils flare in response.

"There it is," he smirks, unbuttoning her fly. "Already so wet for me, little Omega?"

"Shhhh," she pleads, helping him to pull off her jeans. He doesn't bother removing her knickers, flipping her onto her back and tugging himself free, plunging into her in the next moment.

"Alpha," she whimpers and he places his hand over her mouth.

"Quiet little one," he hisses, his thrusts rough, showing her no mercy, taking her quickly to the brink until she's wriggling beneath him, biting his hand to stop herself from screaming.

How does he do it? He always feels so perfect, his body knowing exactly what hers needs.

He follows her soon after, pumping her full, clasping her tightly to him.

"Fuck," he grunts, collapsing onto her as more hot spunk shoots from him. "I'm going to fill your belly with pups, little one. My pups."

She looks at him, twisting her head to get a better view. His face is buried in the pillow, and he pants, his hair wet around his ears. "What?"

He thrusts again with a fresh pulse of spunk. "Doesn't matter."

"But?"

"Alpha crap."

"But do you...do you want to do that?" Ever since she came through puberty, her body has been longing for pups, babies she means. She's not a dog. The idea of being nestled in her strong Alpha's arms with a growing stomach creeps up on her sometimes. And in heat, all she wants is to be fucked full of babies.

It's her dirty secret. To have these fantasies. And to learn he has them too. Unless he's serious that is?

"Fuck, Cora! It's just the inner Alpha talking, you know. Of course, that's all I want to do right now, to you! Fuck, I probably want to do it to you every time I get a whiff of your scent. Do I want a bunch of screaming brats right now? I nearly got kicked out of university. No."

There's a noise in the hallway, the grind of tiny wheels on the floorboards.

"Is she going to stick her head around the door?"

he whispers, lifting up onto his forearms.

"No, I told her I was going to take a nap."

The wheels continue to the end of the hallway, the door opens and the suitcase bumps down the steps and along the path. They hear a car door open and close and the engine starts up before the car pulls away.

Cora lets out a long sigh and he shifts them onto their sides so that he's no longer squashing her.

"Would it be so bad if she knew?" he asks earnestly.

"Because the last time you spoke with Rose ended so well!"

"She was being an aggressive bitch — and you know it. Why does she hate me so much, anyway? The club was the first time I ever spoke to her."

"Do we have to spoil this by talking about that now?"

He stares straight at her. "No."

He snuggles in closer to her, burying his face into her neck until he finds her gland. He can never leave it alone during heat sex. She wishes she had the strength to tell him to stop, but she's too weak for it. He nibbles at her and everything in her brain becomes a blur. Everything is just the scrape of his teeth over her tissue-thin gland, hot and throbbing. Spindles of electricity shoot from the base of her neck down her spine, smouldering out across her body, and she shudders with the glorious sensation. Her body responds to it, and she grinds into him, words flittering from her lips in a muddle of crazed thoughts.

"Bite me, Alpha," she pleads as he kneads her breast with his palm and his fingers.

"Omega!" The word vibrates on her gland and she comes so hard she sees stars.

There's no rest to it. They can't get enough of each other's bodies and they only pause briefly to sleep and eat, Noah ensuring she eats the supplies he's brought and making her drink large glasses of water every hour.

Soon the neatly arranged sheets are a mess of slick and come, sweat and spit, crumbs and stains; all twisted and pulled from the mattress. Their clothes are scattered across the floor, and there's the slightly sweet stink of their souring fluids penetrating the room.

It goes on for three days. His hunger for her never seeming to lessen and his stamina never wavering. It's the same for her, her body exhausted and sore, her hips covered in tiny bruises and her chest scattered with the marks from his mouth, but the deep Omega longing is relentless.

"I want a photo of you like this," he says on the fourth day, the final day of her heat when the fever has begun to wither away, his head between her thighs, lapping lazily at her. She's already peaked and he's teasing her, creeping the tip of his tongue around and around her clit, until she tips over, her cunt spasming with each shock wave. Then he starts all over, keeping her at this dizzying height.

"Photo?" She tenses, pushing away his head

with her hands, trying to hook her leg over his shoulder.

He peers up at her, swiping his arm over his wet chin.

"Yeah. You look amazing when you come."

She scrambles up, tugging the dirty cover with her. "You're not taking my photo."

"Why?" He bounds up the bed, coming to sit next to her. He's still hard, and he palms at himself as his gaze roams over her body.

The way that makes her feel is perplexing. Desired and demeaned both at once.

"You know why."

"I really don't."

"There's no way I'd let you have a photo of me like that! I'm not that dumb."

He frowns. "You think I'd do something bad with it?"

"You haven't exactly got a great track record." She takes a gulp of water from the glass by the bed.

"Actually, I think I've got a pretty good track record. How long have we been doing this exactly? And how many people have I told about it? Zero!"

"There's a reason you haven't told anyone else."

"Yes," he says, "you asked me not to."

"You don't want anyone else knowing too."

"No, Cora. You are the one who doesn't want people to know. I couldn't give a shit."

"You said you didn't want people to know you were sleeping with, I quote, a frigid Omega."

"Fuck, Cora! I don't even remember saying that.

Like I said, I don't have a problem with other people knowing. Why would I? And actually I don't understand why you do." He looks down at the space between them, his hands now limp by his sides, then his eyes travel to meet hers. "Scrap that. I do know why."

"What do you want me to say, Noah? Half my friends would disown me if they knew I was... whatever this is..." she waves her hand through the air between them, "with you, and the other half would think I'd lost my mind."

He twists his head away, one hand fisting the sheet. "Do you actually give a flying toss about me? About my feelings at all?"

His voice is gruff, almost hurt.

Noah hurt? Bullshit! Like he said, he doesn't give a shit about anything. Surely he has no feelings to hurt.

She says that in her mind and instantly knows that it isn't true. There's another side she's seen to him; a more sensitive, kinder one.

But she's also seen his anger. His big Alpha bravado.

Who is the real Noah?

"I don't ... I don't know what I feel." She slumps against the headboard. "Except confused."

The hormones from her heat are fading fast, but she remains fragile, on the edge of tears. The Omega in her would like him to gather her up in his arms and comfort her.

"I thought you liked me," he says it to the carpet

with its worn patches and frayed edges.

She doesn't answer. What can she say? She does like him. And it's a betrayal of everything she stands for, of everything she believes in, and ultimately of herself. Is liking him enough when you stack up everything else that matters too?

"Right," he snaps, labouring off the bed and gathering up his stuff. He doesn't get dressed, instead carries his bundle and his bag out into the hallway and slams the bathroom door behind him.

She sits there stunned, damp with his saliva and his come, insensitive to the tears that start to slip down her cheeks. The bedroom seems like a war zone and she wonders if this is shell shock, a buzzing building in her ears and her vision blurring.

The toilet flushes, and his angry footsteps thunder down the hall, the door whacking open. He doesn't even bother to shut it behind him.

That's it, she thinks, it's over.

It's for the best. Finals are next term and then the start of a whole new life. Maybe she needs to put this whole mess behind her.

Her throat constricts, the breath in her lungs painful. She scrunches up her face and concentrates on breathing.

If it's for the best, why does it feel so wrong?

Slowly, she becomes aware of wetness on her face. She hardly ever cries and when she does it constantly takes her by surprise. The sensation of tears on her cheeks is alien, yet vaguely familiar, as if there was once a time when she cried a lot. Yet, the sadness, the loneliness, that swallows her up like an unexpected storm cloud, its belly a dark and miserable place, is no shock. It seems fitting.

She's used to being alone. It's not new. It's as familiar to her as she assumes love and family are to others. Over the three years she's been here at university, the loneliness has been less acute. She has friends now and belonging; both things she'd been without as a child.

But even then she's known that the loneliness is still there, hovering in the background. A black cloud full of rain, ready to swoop over and drench her at any moment. The holidays have been the worst, when everyone leaves for home. The heats have helped — given her company — but sometimes she's wondered if it really does, because this isolation when he's gone is even more acute. Whenever he picks up his bag and walks out the door, her little Omega soul is desolate from the loss.

Over the next few days she has study and revision to fill her time. Yet it's not enough to distract her or to prevent the cloud of loneliness from sweeping in and releasing its misery on her head.

Her skin is always soaked through, her very soul drenched. Occasionally she has the strength to pull herself up off the floor and dry herself, but it doesn't last long before the rain comes tumbling down again. She tries to focus — focus, focus. To block out everything else, but it is so difficult.

It shouldn't be this difficult, should it? It was just a fling, a casual thing. As meaningless and brief as any other passing cloud.

CHAPTER FIFTEEN

Fuck.

Fuck.

The air is thick and humid. Heavy in his chest, suffocating in his mouth, drowning his tongue. The inside of his throat stings so badly, tears form in his eyes. He swipes his fingers and thumb across his face, squeezing the bridge of his nose.

The pain in his head intensifies, a pressure that might break through his skull. He swerves into an alleyway and hunches over as his body hauls two powerful retches from his belly, and he spits onto the ground.

He revolts her. He's seen it in her eyes so often. He'd tried to pretend it wasn't there. But occasionally he'd spy the flashes of it. He makes her sick. He makes himself sick. He should be here huddling in the shadows puking his guts out.

A sob breaks free from his lips and he leans into the wall. How had he allowed himself to believe otherwise? To fool himself into thinking she cared?

Because she had, hadn't she? He'd seen the glimpses of that too. Not just a sexual attraction or a lust, but something deeper and more solid. Something that he holds reflected in himself.

Now he knows that he must have been deceived. How could someone like Cora care for someone like him?

Someone so good could not like someone so bad. And that's the nub of it. She's like everyone else. After everything, she still views him as the monster they all say he is. He scares her. He is too big, too clumsy, he doesn't fit anywhere.

Now he has made the mistake of letting her penetrate into the very heart of him, and he will be haunted by the little beams of happiness they've shared. And every time they pop unbidden into his mind he'll have to relive the pain all over again.

They come rushing into his head now, a torrent of water through a crack.

Cora slipping her small hand into his.

Cora laughing so hard she clutches her stomach when he said something funny.

Cora with her sweet lips wrapped around his cock, her eyes closed in pleasure.

The colour of her eyes, the softness of her skin, the pressure of her weight, the sound of her moans: they run through his mind, taunting him, and he heaves a third time.

People pass the end of the alley, oblivious to

him. He stays there, allowing himself this moment of grief, hoping that he can vomit her out of his system, and then he wipes his face on his sleeve and heads home.

After a shower, he throws his belongings into a bag and cycles to the train station, locking up his bike, and catching a train to London. He has no idea if his parent's will be home — he hasn't spoken to them for weeks, but he doesn't care. He wants to be far away from the university.

The house his parents own stands in an exclusive central London square, where the tall, white townhouses ring a neatly kept enclosure of grass, encircled by metal railings that get locked at night. Many of the four-storey houses have been divided up into flats or office space; there's a think tank, several law firms, and a private doctor's clinic. His parents' house is one of the few that retains all its floors for one house. Even the basement belongs to them — converted into a space for Noah that he can access down a set of steps from the street.

Ideally, he'd like to head straight down there and go to bed. It's only mid afternoon, but he's battered and drained — like it wasn't Cora's words that hurt him but her fists. He can almost imagine that she beat them against his chest. It feels bruised. But he should say hi, so he climbs the two wide steps and opens the polished door. The alarm isn't on, so he dumps his bag in the hallway by the coat stand and goes to find out who is home. It's unlikely to be his mother at this hour; it is probably the cleaner or the chef that comes a couple of times a week.

The large sitting room with its plush cream carpet and expensive art work is empty and so is the study and the TV room. The dining room is only ever used for dinner parties and Christmas day, so he heads to the rear of the house to the extended part where the kitchen is situated. It runs the whole width of the building and the cleaner is needed to keep its polished marble surfaces glistening.

He finds his dad hovering at the breakfast bar, hunched over his laptop. He's got his earphones on and his back to the door so he doesn't see Noah until he taps him on the shoulder.

The older man glances up and beams. He's tall like Noah, though not as broad. As a young man he was a long-distance runner and he retains the willowy frame. His hair is cropped close to his head, but Noah sees that he's greyer than when they last met, almost white around the ears. He has the same face as Noah's older brother but his dad's is lined. His dad smiles a lot, especially for an Alpha. He is quietly relaxed in himself, self assured, confident and easy going — qualities Noah has not inherited.

"Ah, Noah boy," he twists on his stall and slaps Noah on the back. "I didn't know we were expecting you."

Noah sits on the chair next to him. "It was a last

minute decision. I decided I'd get more revision done here."

His dad pats him on the shoulder again. "Wonderful to have you home, son." He grins and his nostrils flair. His father cocks his head to one side. "Hmmm, same girl, huh? Must be getting serious."

Noah shakes his head. "Nah, it's not."

"Good thing too," his dad laughs. "Bit young to become tied down just yet. You've got to have your fun while you can. Plenty of Omegas out there, and these days you can help them out without any ramifications. God, to have had it that way in my youth. The suppressants and birth control weren't as effective. Lots of unwanted pregnancies."

A heat runs through Noah's body and he can't look at his dad. Instead, he lets his eyes wander about the kitchen, waiting for the emotion to pass.

"Women, especially Omegas, are pretty exhausting in my experience," Noah says.

"I bet they are."

They've had this conversation many times since Noah had his first rut. His dad seems to want to live his own missed opportunities through him.

Noah smiles weakly, wanting to change the subject but unsure how.

If his dad assumes it would be so great to sleep around, he wonders why he never has. Well, he's pretty sure he hasn't. The whole scent thing makes it virtually impossible to get away with an affair when you're an Alpha or an Omega.

"Where's Mum?"

"The office. She's out tonight though — won't be home until late."

"What you working on?"

"I'm not. I submitted my column already. I'm trying to clear some emails."

His dad is a commentator for the Times but the truth is he doesn't need to work — his mum and his dad both come from wealth.

"I'd better go dump my stuff in my room." Noah says after a pause.

"God, yes. You know your mum throws a fit if she finds your stuff scattered about."

It's why they moved him to the basement; his mother can't stand his scent all over the rest of the house.

The self-contained flat in the basement is much as he left it. The cleaner has obviously been in there a few times, everything is cleaned and the pile of clothes he dropped on the floor has been laundered and folded on his bed.

The retro record player he bought himself sits untouched in the corner with his records stacked alongside, next to a 1970s vintage leather recliner, a pair of headphones hung over the arm. They were too precious to take to university. He'd taken his smart speakers and TV instead.

On the walls are pinned posters that he's outgrown: a few topless girls, his rugby team and some of his favourite bands. He's brought a few girls back over the years. He examines the room and cringes. What was he thinking?

There's a small shower room and toilet down here as well as a kitchenette. But the fridge has been unplugged along with the microwave and there's nothing to eat.

He's starving. Post-rut he always is, and he hasn't eaten since Cora's. His stomach growls angrily, but he ignores it and the gnawing inside and lies out flat on the ground, allowing his body to sink against the cold wooden floorboards. Her smell lingers on his skin, no wonder his dad could smell it. He'd scrubbed himself raw in the shower earlier, enjoying the fierce scrape of the flannel and the sting of the soap. But it wasn't enough. She's still there. It's some cruel torture. He closes his eyes and tries not to think of her.

CHAPTER
SIXTEEN

"Step away from the laptop!" Zach says, flinging open her bedroom door dramatically.

Cora lifts her hands above her head and stretches.

"Hi Zach. When did you get back to Oxford?"

"Last night." He still has a bandage wrapped around his hand, but it's a lot smaller than it was. "Come on, like I said, step away from that desk. I'm kidnapping you for the day."

"To do what?"

"Hang out with me and Rose." Rose appears behind him, her bag slung over her shoulder. She returned from her trip a couple of days ago too.

"Zach, I can't! It's only twenty-one days until my first exam."

"When was the last time you took a break?"

"I take a break every day to sleep."

"Apart from 'to sleep'?"

She crosses her arms across her chest and glares at him. There's no time for breaks. She starts revising as soon as she wakes in the morning and doesn't stop until bedtime. Finals start at the beginning of the summer term. The six exams she has to sit will determine whether she passes or fails her degree. She's drafted herself a timetable and made a list of everything she needs to re-read and all the arguments she should commit to memory. There is no room to screw up; a degree will give her the security she needs.

"Oh come on Cora, just for a few hours," Rose says, stepping inside her room and coming to take her hand. "It's a beautiful day out there and it will do you good."

"I'm not leaving until you agree, so if you want to get back to studying you may as well concede quickly."

"Fine, fine," Cora says, letting Rose drag her to her feet. She grabs her phone, her keys and her debit card and follows them out of the flat. "So what we doing?"

"We could go to the Crown. It's got a nice garden?"

"I'm not drinking," Cora says.

Zach rolls his eyes. "Okay, Saint Cora."

"How about punting?" Rose says as they stroll along the busy pavement. "I've nearly finished my time here and I've never actually been punting."

"How is that possible?" Zach asks.

Rose shrugs. "I don't know."

"Right, let's do that then."

"It'll be packed on the river today," Cora grumbles. It's a sunny May day, the sky a bright blue, not a cloud in sight and the trees full to bursting with blossom.

Rose and Zach ignore her and they weave down the side streets and out to Magdalen Bridge, joining the end of the queue for people waiting to hire a punt.

"Isn't hiring a punt expensive?" Cora says, chewing her nail.

"Matt from college works here — look." Zach points him out, a tall scrawny boy with a thick mop of blonde hair. "I hear he'll give us a discount."

The line moves quickly and soon they reach the river edge. Zach slaps Matt's hand, and he helps them into the flat-bottomed boat with its squared ends.

"You know how to do this?" Matt asks.

"Yes," Zach and Cora say together.

"I have to give you life jackets, but nobody ever wears them. You can shove them under the seats." He passes them the three orange vests and then gives Zach the long quant pole. "You have an hour."

Cora takes a seat next to Rose as Zach pushes away from the bank and down the river, striking out straight into a backlog of other punters on the water. His steering is hazardous and twice they bump into other boats, the punt rocking madly and Rose yelping.

"Let me do it." Cora stands and stretches out her hands.

"Happily," says Zach, peering at the side of the

punt. "I don't want to lose my deposit and it's hurting my hand."

Carefully, Cora makes her way to the stern of the punt and takes the pole from Zach, and he stumbles into the seat. The boat rocks again and Rose clamps her eyes shut.

"Right," Cora says, plunging the pole down into the water till the end hits the sticky bottom of the river. Using her weight, she pushes off, driving the boat forward, then lifts the pole, so it trails in the water behind them and uses it as a rudder, guiding their boat through the maze of novice punters and along the river.

Trees, dense with fresh leaves, line the banks, their branches creeping across the river, creating a canopy of foliage and turning the water a murky green. Sunshine seeps through the gaps and the water is dappled in patches of shadow and light. They glide over the surface of the water, faint ripples following in their wake.

For a moment they are quiet, happy to bob along, soaking up the view and watching the people they float by.

"I wish we had snacks," Cora says, gazing across to a punt parked up by the bank; the four tourists inside sharing punnets of strawberries and passing around a bottle of champagne.

"I have some Reese's cups my mom brought me from home." Rose rummages in her bag.

Cora sticks out her tongue. "No thanks."

"I'll have some." Zach says. He pops one in his

mouth and says, with his mouth full, "So what's everyone's news?"

"News? I've been studying non-stop," Cora scoffs. "All I've been thinking about is goddamn philosophy and politics." Well, that and Noah. At night she's exhausted, yet she lies on her back staring at the ceiling, trying not to think of him, trying not to feel regret. She shakes those thoughts away now. "I've even started dreaming about it. Last night I dreamt I was dating the Prime Minister."

"How about you, Rose?"

Rose chews rapidly. "I can show you more of my holiday photos."

"Err, no thanks." He dips his hand in the water. "Oh, wait. I have some gossip." He looks up at them both. "Remember that girl who sent those dodgy photos to all the dudes on the University rugby team? She's done it again. Only this time it was her tutor."

"Oh my God!" Rose shrieks.

Cora stares at him, her skin suddenly cold. "Wait, what? She sent those photos to everyone on the team?"

Zach grins. "Okay, maybe that was an exaggeration, it was about four or five of them."

Her arms drop by her sides and she nearly loses the pole into the water.

"Careful," Rose calls out.

Cora rubs her temple. "But I thought she sent the photo to only Noah, and he passed it on."

"No, she sent them to a whole load of dudes at once. I think her name is Sarah. There's obviously something a bit wrong with her," Zach says.

She thought that the girl, Sarah, and Noah had been dating. She thought he'd passed around the photos. Wasn't that the story? But he'd said he'd never dated an Omega, hadn't he? And now she considers it, she's never smelled his scent mixed with another woman's. In the early days of their arrangement, she'd just assumed he was sleeping with other people. But she's only ever smelt his scent, his strong woody scent, his scent alone.

She sits down hard, her legs like jelly.

"You alright, Cora?" Rose asks.

"Y-yes," she stutters, "Just taking a break."

"Have you been into college yet?" Rose says, unwrapping another chocolate.

Cora shakes her head and Zach says, "Not yet."

"There's something going on." Rose scrapes the chocolate from the surface of the Reese's cup with her teeth. "The mood was, I don't know, weird. Sombre even."

"What do you mean?" Zach wipes his wet hands on his jeans.

"The second years are all here early. They were hovering around in groups, whispering and hugging each other. Some were sobbing."

"Sounds like something happened."

Rose nods. "Yeah. The staff were acting differently too. Even Jack the porter looked worried. He wasn't his usual chirpy self at all."

"I guess we'll hear about it on the grapevine soon enough," Zach says, helping himself to more chocolate.

It's Wednesday Cora finds out.

She turns up for her shift at the cafe and sees. Someone's left the local newspaper on a table.

University assault

She picks the paper up and slides it under the counter. In her ten minute break, she takes it out back and sits on the fold-up chair in the office, scanning the article. An Omega was attacked walking home; two Alphas jumping her from behind. Luckily some passersby intervened before they could cause her any further damage but she's still in the hospital with a cracked skull.

The words swim before Cora's eyes and she feels sick. An Omega attacked? She recognises the name of the girl. Some sweet, quiet scientist who sometimes comes along to the talks on Omega rights. She never contributes much, but she's always willing to sign any petition going. Cora heard she had a Beta boyfriend. Is that why the Alphas targeted her? There are some militant types who don't believe in inter-designation relationships like that. Or more likely, they are your usual Alpha predators.

The article says that no arrests have been made, although the police are talking to some Alpha students. Anybody with information has been asked to come forward.

There's also a column written by one of the

girl's friends. It's a continuation of the stuff spouted after the nightclub incident between Noah and Zach. According to the author, this incident was a tragedy waiting to happen. Alphas are a menace; their actions should be better scrutinised and greater safety controls put in place for the protection of others. Controls like the new-to-the-market drugs that help to fiercely suppress an Alpha's instincts and behaviours. She fails to mention the side effects that are associated with this type of medication, the ones that make it very unpopular with Alphas.

Cora doesn't agree with it. She is definitely for increasing and protecting the rights of Omegas, but not at the price of restricting the rights of Alphas.

Folding up the paper and placing it in the recycling bin, she returns to work and only later when she picks up her rucksack at the end of her shift does she consider catching the bus home instead of walking.

CHAPTER SEVENTEEN

He doesn't think anything of it when the police officers arrive at his student house the first day of term and ask him to come to the station for a chat. He assumes they're talking to all the Alphas, searching for leads, finding out what people know.

They arrive when he's fresh out of the shower and sit waiting in the filthy communal kitchen while he dresses. Then they take him away in an unmarked car; the two police officers riding in the front while he hunches in the back. The car is small for his frame and his neck aches as they move slowly through the city, the traffic dense with morning commuters. Students swarm on the pavements as they pass the university, and fat raindrops begin to hit the windscreen.

The police station is familiar.The smell of lemon cleaning fluids and alcohol still hang on the walls and the floor. He'd spent hours here, locked in a cell after that first fight.

Yet, despite that previous experience, it never

occurs to him to ask for a lawyer. It's only when he's sat on an uncomfortably small chair in a plain box room on one side of a plastic table that a creeping sensation skims along his skin and he begins to sweat.

He's got nothing to worry about, has he? Kyle told him about the assault, although he'd heard a brief mention of it on the national news the week before. He'd groaned, knowing it would be more ammunition for the anti-Alpha brigade, and an instinctual concern for his Omega, Cora, had spiralled through his nervous system. (Not his Omega, he reminded himself with sorrow). But after that he hadn't given it much consideration; he'd been more concerned about last minute revision.

So how has he ended up here, opposite two grimly dressed police inspectors? They are both Betas — one a middle aged woman with her bleached hair scraped into a bun at the base of her head, and the other a squat younger man who frowns so severely Noah is sure he must be giving himself a headache.

The woman does most of the questioning while her colleague alternates between taking notes and glaring. Between them, a recording machine blinks a red light ominously.

The questions and the tone of their talk started off friendly, as if he was doing them a big favour by volunteering to come and chat with them and help solve this crime. But now he's pretty sure he's in a whole heap of shit. If only he'd stop sweating.

Innocent people don't sweat, he's making himself look guilty and he's not. The only problem is he has no alibi — not one he can use, anyway. He was in the city when the assault took place, with his phone switched off, and he won't tell them why.

He squirms on the seat, hitting his knees on the table when the woman, Inspector Browne, asks him if he can account for his movements on 23rd April and can explain why his mobile was turned off for the duration of that afternoon and the next three days. For the third time, he stares at the inspector blankly.

What should he say? He'd promised Cora he wouldn't tell anyone about their time together. Surely, he can break that promise in this circumstance? But the prospect of doing that has his chest aching. The information would spread like wildfire, and he can't bring himself to betray her like that. Even if it hurts him, even if it feels like a dagger in his heart. The thought of being his disgusts her so much she can't bear for others to know.

So what does he do? Lie? The clock on the far wall ticks loudly, the second hand whizzing alarmingly quickly around the clock face. Both inspectors wait. The man taps his pen on the table-top.

Noah swallows.

"I'd like to speak to a lawyer, please," he says.

"You're just helping us with our enquiries. It's really not necessary," the older inspector says with a smile that doesn't reach her eyes.

Noah crosses his arms and stares straight ahead.

"It won't look good for you, if you don't cooperate. You got something to hide, Noah?" the young man sneers. It almost sounds like a threat. Noah concentrates on the small piece of blue tack he can see stuck to the wall behind the inspectors. It's lost its bright blue colour, now so faint it's almost translucent. He won't lose his temper. He won't think about the colour blue and Cora's eyes either. How they'd be filled with disappointment.

He rings his mother when they finally let him have his phone call. There had been some further wrangling, some persuasion that he didn't need one and then some talk that veered close to bullying, but he stood firm, refusing to say anything more.

His mother is, of course, the last person he wants to call but also the only person he can. She is a very, very good lawyer after all and would scare the shit out of the lot of them here.

"Hi Mum," he says.

"Noah, hi, I'm in the middle of something here, darling. Can we talk later?"

"No. This is urgent."

She sighs. "Darling, I am very busy—"

"I've been arrested."

He hears her shift in her chair and can picture her face, her forehead creased with concern.

"Tell me."

So he does and she listens, not speaking until he gets to the end.

"Don't speak to anyone again. I'm on my way, darling. I'm leaving now." Then she hangs up.

He wonders if she thinks he did it. She never asked.

Turns out the cell at the police station is just as he remembers, too. A white tiled room, a stainless-steel toilet in the corner and a hard bench. He can't believe he's back here. The last time, he'd sworn with everything he had that he'd never end up in a mess like that again. He'd work solidly on his control and his anger. He was never coming back.

And, shit, he has worked hard. He's walked away from so many goddamn fights, trained seriously, studied loads; he's even been in something closely resembling a steady relationship. But what for? Here he is again.

Outside his cell, he hears a mixture of heavy booted footsteps, hushed tones and pained shouting. The man in the cell next to him seems high, pacing backward and forward, rattling the door, screaming obscenities. It's not only the noise that attacks his senses, the stench is noxious: urine, sweat, bleach — the powerfully industrial kind that seems to burn the fine hairs in his nasal passages.

Bunching over his lap, he tries to breathe through his mouth and count calmly like they'd taught him, concentrating all his focus on each number, the way it sounds and looks in his head. At two hundred he realises with a jolt that it's not his own voice he hears, but Cora's — soothing, comforting — he desperately clings to that, not letting the other feelings overtake him.

CHAPTER EIGHTEEN

On her way into the students' union's communal kitchen, Cora finds Zach studying at one of the tables near the entrance.

"Hey lovely," he says, grinning, although he looks tired. "How're you?"

"Fine," she says, wrapping her arms around him and kissing his cheek. "How's the hand?

"The hand's fine. It's my head that's killing me today." As she steps away, he kneads his temples.

"Too much revision? You want me to make you a cuppa?" Cora asks, heading for the kettle. He doesn't answer and she turns back to find him observing her. "Do you want a cup of tea?"

"No, no... I mean, yes, actually I would."

Cora laughs. "You sound frazzled."

"No... it's... they've made some arrests for the assault."

"Shit, really?" Cora halts with the box of tea bags in her hands. "That is a relief." She places the box next to the bubbling kettle and reaches up into the cupboard for two mugs.

"It's university students."

"What?"

"I feel... responsible."

"Responsible? Why?"

"I could've stopped it from happening."

"You? How?"

"I should've let them kick him out of the university."

Cora freezes. The mug in her right hand slips from her fingers and plummets to the floor. The china smashes into pieces.

"Noah?" she whispers.

"What?"

"You mean, Noah?"

"Yes, they've arrested Noah." Zach shakes his head. "I should never have defended him. The dude is clearly a sicko, a psychopath."

Cora's legs tremble and she leans against the counter for support.

Words form in her mind, but somehow they don't make it to her mouth. Noah? Why have they arrested Noah?

"Everyone's in uproar," Zach says, gesturing to his laptop.

Cora drops to the floor, gathering up the pieces of the broken cup along with her thoughts.

"But... but I don't understand," she says.

"What do you mean?" Zach asks, passing her some sheets of old newspaper from among his books.

She takes it and wraps the shards of china. "Didn't the assault take place that first Sunday of the holidays?"

"Yes, why?"

"I...." She lifts the bin lid with a snap of her foot and throws the bundle inside.

Zach passes her a dustpan and brush, and Cora crouches down and sweeps the fragments of the broken cup into the pan. Her hands tremble and she's lightheaded, her vision blurring so that she's forced to focus hard on her actions. She stands, opening the bin again and angling the pan so the pieces slide into the bag. Then she spins around and walks out, vaguely aware of Zach calling her. She hurries along the corridor and down the staircase, only realising the pan and brush remain in her hands as she steps into the bright sunshine. She drops them by her feet.

Above her there is not a wisp of a cloud in the sky nor a breath of wind in the air, the morning's rain clouds and the earlier puddles vanquished. It seems wrong. It is a day when good things should happen. Happy, joyful things. Instead, the heat from the sun beats down on her head like a spotlight, watching her, waiting to see what she'll do.

She looks down at her feet and her toes wriggle independently. They could turn left and take her home. Noah didn't do it. There is no need for her to get involved. They'll let him go, she can stay out of it.

But that's not her. She believes in doing the

right thing. She takes a step forward and then another. The police station is not somewhere she's ever wanted to go or to be. But she can go and talk to them and nobody else need ever know. Her feet keep moving.

The old Victorian police station is built of red brickwork and squat dimensions. As she arrives at the doors they slide open automatically and the unsavoury smells from within assault her nose. She holds her breath and steps inside the darkness. There's a counter, but it isn't manned, and there's no buzzer or bell. Nobody else is there, and she waits impatiently, chewing on her bottom lip. Finally, a man in uniform emerges from a room behind. He sees her but he doesn't come over straight away, first straightening up some paperwork.

"Can I help?" he asks after several minutes.

"Is Noah Wood here? They said he'd been arrested for the Omega assault."

The policeman is losing his hair and he's cut what remains very short. The sharp bristles catch the electric light as he lowers his chin to eye her.

"You a journalist?" he says.

"What? No, I—"

"I can't disclose information about an ongoing investigation."

"I have information about the case. Noah didn't do it — he was with me."

The man's grey eyes narrow. "You're an Omega, aren't you? Are you *his* Omega?"

Cora straightens. "Excuse me?"

"We get Omegas in here all the time, giving us fake alibis and wasting our time. You understand wasting police time is an offence?"

"I'm not wasting your time. I'm telling the truth!" She tries to say it firmly, but she can hear the note of desperation in her voice.

The police officer smirks at her. Behind him, the red beam of a video camera blinks.

"I want to talk to the investigating officers," Cora hisses through her teeth.

"They're busy."

"How about your supervisor then," she glances at the man's badge, "Constable Lock."

"She's at lunch," he says flatly. Then picks up a pen and clicks the point down. "Look, I'll tell you what I'll do, I'll take down your name and phone number and that gives you a bit of time to think about whether you actually want to do this."

Cora pauses. "No."

The man nods and places down his pen.

"I'll come back." The police officer goes to say something, but she doesn't let him. "With a lawyer."

She turns and strides away, out into the street. Yes, she needs a lawyer. A lawyer she can trust. She needs Rose.

Cora sprints the whole way home, sweaty and red faced by the time she rushes through the front door. She pauses, hunching forward and heaving deep breaths. She's been so desperate to get here, she hasn't planned what she's going to say. How will she explain everything to Rose? And will she even help? Rose hates Noah.

Running her arm across her damp brow, she takes one last deep swallow and heads to Rose's room, knocking lightly and then entering.

"Hi Cora," Rose says, spinning around to face the doorway. Classical music plays quietly in the background and, above her desk, a pin board has been fixed to the wall covered in revision notes and diagrams. On the floor there are neatly arranged piles of textbooks and A4 bind folders. Rose cocks her head. "You okay, sweetie?"

"No. I'm not, Rose." She steps inside, her friend's sweet scent strong in the room. Behind her back, she twists her hands. Where to start?

"Is it the news? You heard, right? about them arresting those guys?"

Cora nods.

"It's hard to believe that someone we actually know would do—"

"Rose," she says sternly, "Noah didn't do it."

She looks straight at her friend, eyes not wavering from hers. Rose peers at her with curiosity.

"How do you know?"

Cora's head spins. There's a lot of ringing in her ears and Rose's face swims in front of her.

"Because he was with me."

"With you? What? Did you see him that night or something?"

"No. He was with me, with me. We were sharing a heat."

Rose's mouth opens, but she says nothing.

If only Rose were an Omega or an Alpha, she could read her scent better, understand what she thinks, what she feels. She closes her eyes, she has a headache building.

"You shared your heat with Noah, Noah Wood?"

"Yes," Cora says.

"Noah? Did he bully you into it, Cora? Alphas can't do stuff like that anymore."

"It was a hundred percent consensual."

"Oh." Rose collapses back against her chair. "So like a mutual heat arrangement thing."

Cora takes a deep gulp of air and turns to close the door, unable to face Rose when she replies. "Actually, it's more than just that. We've been seeing each other."

"What the!" Rose gasps. "For how long?"

"I... I don't know. We've been sharing my heat for a while, but I guess it developed into something more than that after Christmas."

"But you never told me."

"No." Cora twists round towards Rose. Her friend's eyes are full of hurt and confusion, and a sudden sickness surges through Cora's body.

"It was a secret?" Rose says. "Was that his idea?"

"No, mine."

"But why?"

"I dont know." She slides down the door, crumpling onto the floor and burying her face in her hands. "I guess I was worried what people would think."

"Really? I didn't take you for someone who cared about that, Cora."

She leans in harder to her hands, letting that shame and guilt swallow her up. "I do," she says quietly.

"But I don't understand, is it like a sex thing or more than that?"

The realisation creeps in. She's known it for a long time in the depths of her mind, but she's not allowed herself to truly acknowledge it until now. But now she knows for certain that her feelings for Noah are a lot stronger than sex, than some physical thing between them. It goes much deeper than that, as if he's touched something sacred and hidden within her and kicked it into being.

"It's much, much more than that," she admits, removing her hands as her lip trembles.

"Then what are you going to do about it?"

"Do?"

"Your boyfriend, or whatever he is, has been arrested?"

Shit. Yes. That.

"Have the police been in touch about his alibi?" Rose says.

"No. He won't have told them."

"Because it was a secret?"

"Yes," she says, bowing her head. "And I've just been down there and the officer at the desk wouldn't even listen to me."

"But his mobile phone will show he was nowhere near the crime scene."

"I always make him turn it off. Fuck, it's going to look bad for him."

"Yes, it is."

"And they don't believe me." Her voice rises in panic. "They think I'm his Omega and that I'm just covering for him. Shit, they probably think I'm saying it out of some Alpha-Omega loyalty thing. Especially if he changes his story because of me."

"Is there any way you can prove he was with you?"

She racks her brains desperately trying to figure out some way of connecting him to her, to her home. She shakes her head violently. "No, no. There's nothing."

"Hmmm, there might be one way. You might not like it though."

"What?" Cora asks.

" I have studied some case law where swabs were done on an Omega which showed they'd been in heat so many days ago and with a certain Alpha; DNA evidence."

"Would that work time wise?"

"It did in those cases, but I'm not sure."

Cora jumps to her feet. "That sounds hopeful," she says. "I'd better get back down there."

"Wait, wait. Slow down, Cora. You shouldn't go down there without a lawyer."

"A lawyer?" she says. Yes, that's why she's here. She needs Rose by her side, someone that knows the game and the rules and how to play.

"Yes. The police are notorious for their Alpha

Omega prejudice. You need someone with you who knows the law. Otherwise, it could all blow up in your face."

"I can't afford a lawyer! Can *you* help me please, Rose?"

Rose shakes her head, and the earth falls away beneath Cora's feet.

But then Rose pulls out her phone. "Let me call my tutor. She's an expert in Omega law. I'm sure she'd help."

"Seriously?"

"Well, let's see." Rose lifts the phone to her ear and Cora can hear it ringing, then a clipped, female voice answers. Rose explains the situation, and Cora can't help but be impressed by her friend. From her it would have been a rambling mess, but from Rose it's clear, precise and persuasive.

"She wants to talk to you," Rose says, handing over the phone.

"Hello," Cora says, cradling the phone against her cheek.

"Hello, this is Dr Pearson. Ms Swift?"

"Yes. Hi,"

"Ms Swift, I am willing to help you, but before I do, I have to ask you whether what you have told Rose is the truth. Were you with Mr Wood on the night of the assault?"

"Yes, that's correct. I was."

"And that is the absolute truth?"

"Yes," she says firmly.

"In that case, this is what we are going to do:

I will call the station to tell them we are coming in to make a statement. I will arrange a time and will text you the details. I will meet you outside the station. Do not, under any circumstances, go in there without me. Do you understand — even if they invite you in?"

"Ok, yes. But will it be soon? I can't bear," she pauses to stop her voice from wavering, "for him to be stuck in there when he did nothing wrong."

"I expect they'll want this done as soon as possible. If he has an alibi, it makes no sense for them to waste any more time on Mr Wood."

"Ok."

"Now what's your number?"

Cora recites it off and Dr Pearson reassures her she'll be in touch shortly, then hangs up. When Cora looks back to Rose, she sees she has made her a cup of tea. She hands it over and they go to sit around the kitchen table.

"She's going to help?" Rose asks.

Cora nods. "She's calling the station and arranging a time for me to go in and make a statement."

"Good. She's amazing."

"Thanks, Rose." She squeezes her friend's hand. "Really thank you."

"So, now. Are you going to tell me how the hell you ended up in a thing with Noah Wood?"

CHAPTER
NINETEEN

Dr Pearson is a small, slight woman with a practical but unflattering haircut and unfashionable rectangular glasses. She wears a suit despite the warm day, and beside her Cora wishes she'd worn a more professional outfit rather than the yellow sundress she'd thrown on.

She meets her outside the police station and the tutor leads her to a coffee shop. As they go inside and find a table, Cora looks around and spies men and women dressed in suits, and she's sure this must be a regular place for lawyers to meet their clients. Her right hand shakes and she stuffs it out of sight on her lap as she takes her seat.

They order a coffee each and then Dr Pearson heads straight for the crux of the matter, not bothering with small talk. "I need you to run through the timeline of events," she says, taking out a small moleskin notebook, and popping the cap from her expensive looking fountain pen.

Cora swallows, looking around. It's not something she wants strangers to hear.

Dr Pearson leans forward and smiles sympathetically. "First things first. Don't be embarrassed about this or ashamed or any other nonsense emotion. You've done nothing wrong and you are helping catch the real perpetrator by setting the matter straight. Do you understand, Cora? This is the right thing to do."

Cora nods. "Yes." She takes a deep breath. "Noah —the Alpha they've arrested."

Dr Pearson nods briskly and waves her hand.

"Arrived on the Sunday and stayed with me," she lowers her voice, "helping me through my heat, until the Thursday."

"And he didn't leave you at all during that time?"

Cora raises her eyebrows.

"I know, I know, silly question, Cora, but one you will be asked."

"No. There were moments when we both slept or he made me food. But the evening that attack took place was right at the start of my heat and at that point I was very much awake and," heat rises in her cheeks, "and he was very much with me."

"Good. You need to say it like that. With that conviction. Don't let them bully or intimidate you," the law tutor scribbles in her book. "And there is no way in the confusion of your heat, you could've been muddled about the timing, et cetera?"

"No. He arrived on Sunday lunchtime and we

didn't sleep until late that night, until after the assault had happened."

"And the business with the phone?"

"I always make him give me his phone and I switch it off."

"Yes," she closes her book, "I can see how his phone being switched off would look suspicious to the police."

Cora runs her hands down her face.

"Don't worry, though, Cora." The woman pats her shoulder. "I'm confident this won't take long." She turns in her seat to put on her jacket. "Oh, one other thing. How long have you had this arrangement with this Alpha?"

Cora stares at her. How long? She counts. It can't be that long, can it? "Eighteen months."

"Right, so there'll be a pattern which will help." The older woman stands up and drains her cup and Cora follows, leaving her own drink untouched. She follows Dr Pearson down the street and across the road, her heart pounding in her chest and in her ears.

A different police officer, this time a young woman, greets them from behind the desk and shows them along a corridor to a plain room where two police inspectors are waiting for them.

Dr Pearson continues her equally efficient manner. She dismisses the inspectors' offers of cups of tea and their attempts to needle bits of information from Cora and takes charge of the conversation.

"We're here to make a statement," she says. "Inspector Browne, I explained the situation on the phone. We would like to help you with your investigation."

The inspectors glance at each other.

"Thank you," says the middle aged woman. "We are just trying to understand the nature of Ms Swift and Mr Wood's relationship."

Under the table, Cora wrings her hands. Up until a couple of hours ago nobody else knew about this 'relationship'. Now she's going to have to define it to two hostile strangers.

"Why doesn't Ms Swift tell you what she knows first and then you ask any questions afterwards? I think it would save us all a great deal of time."

"Okay," says Inspector Browne. "Please go ahead?"

Cora coughs. The male inspector is eyeing her with a grim expression so she directs herself towards the woman.

"On the first week of the Easter holidays—"

"What week was that?"

"The week commencing 23rd April," Dr Pearson says.

"I had scheduled my heat. I always schedule them for the holidays so as not to interfere with my studies." She peers down at the plain table. Its surface is plastic, but it's made to appear wooden. "Noah has been helping me with my heats for about a year and a half. He was with me for nearly the whole of that week and didn't leave my flat."

"Let's be certain about this," the man says. "When did he arrive and when did he leave?"

"He arrived on the Sunday, Sunday 23rd, and left on Thursday 27th."

"And you were together the whole time? How can you be certain he didn't leave?"

Cora looks at Dr Pearson, who gestures for her to continue. She stares the man hard in the eye, determined not to be ashamed of her actions. They are normal, perfectly normal, Dr Pearson had said. She likes that woman a lot. "We were together in my flat for that whole period of time . He didn't leave, that would be kind of impossible for an Alpha to do in the middle of a rut with an Omega in heat."

"Mr Wood has been vague about his whereabouts at the time of the assault," Inspector Brown says.

"I asked him to keep our arrangement private."

"But given the circumstance, I suspect he would—"

"Ms Swift can show you the correspondence leading up to their planned time together," Dr Pearson interjects.

"The point is Mr Wood didn't reveal this to us, and we also have the added problem that his mobile phone was switched off for the whole time of the assault."

"I took his phone off him when he arrived and switched it off. An Omega can be quite vulnerable during a heat and that made me feel more secure."

She doesn't need to say more; the internet is full of pictures of Omegas during heats that have clearly been taken without their consent.

"I assume the phone records would show Mr Wood arriving at Ms Swift's and his phone showing at that same location again when he left on the 27th," Dr Pearson adds.

Inspector Browne signals at the other policeman and he opens the file in front of him and shuffles through the papers, locating a sheet that he pulls out and scans his eyes over.

"Please confirm your address," he says.

"Flat 1, Number 10, Newbeem Road, OX1 3XY."

The inspector pulls out a printed map and runs his hand over it, locating the address and sweeping his gaze over the area.

"Yes, we'd need to double check, but the records do seem to confirm that."

Cora exhales silently, her shoulders relaxing. Dr Pearson presses her hand under the table.

"Is there anything else you need from Ms Swift?"

The inspectors look to one another and the younger man shakes his head.

"No, that's all," says Inspector Browne. "We'll take a note of your phone number and get in touch with you if we need to."

Dr Pearson fishes a business card out of her breast pocket. "I'd appreciate it if you'd call me in such a case."

The inspector takes the card somewhat sheepishly.

"Does this mean you'll let him go?" Cora says.

The inspector sighs, tucking the business card into the file. "Yes."

Cora bites her lip, caught by an urge to burst into tears and start hugging everyone in the room. Instead she steadies herself and whispers, "thank you."

Outside the station, she shakes Dr Pearson's hand.

"Well, that was relatively straightforward. And I'm pleased we saved you the need for a swab analysis," the tutor says.

"I have a suspicion it wouldn't have gone so easily without you there."

The small lady smiles, gripping Cora's hands in her own. "I wish the two of you the best of luck, and if the police do get in touch, call me."

"I will."

"I have to dash back to the office now. Can I drop you anywhere?"

"No, thank you. I'm going to wait here."

The older woman nods. "Take care," she tells her as she leaves.

CHAPTER TWENTY

At the count of seven thousand and twenty-two, a pair of footsteps halt outside his cell and the lock rattles in the door before it slides open. A uniformed officer waits by the door.

"I'm pleased to tell you, Mr Wood, that you are no longer a suspect and therefore free to go," the man tells him

"What?"

"You can leave. A few papers you need to sign first. Your parents are waiting for you at the front desk."

He nods and stands, running his hand through his hair and straightening his t-shirt.

His mum is better than he thought she was. He glances at his watch. She can't have got here more than half an hour ago, and already he's free.

His dad waits for him at the reception desk, looking relieved. He steps forward when he sees Noah and grasps him by the shoulders.

"You alright, son?" he asks.

"Yes, fine." Around him his dad's scent peaks with concern, and the intensity of it along with his dad's worried eyes finally lets the severity of everything sink in. He coughs and his dad squeezes. "Where's Mum?"

"Talking to the inspector in charge, trying to find out what's going on."

"I don't understand."

"When we got here, your mother was ready to go all guns blazing, and then they told us you are no longer under arrest."

Noah squeezes the bridge of his nose. "What the fuck?" he mutters.

"Must be some new information."

A small constable behind the desk slides a clear plastic bag onto the counter, containing his keys, wallet and phone. "Here's your belongings, Mr Wood. Please could you sign for them?"

Noah scribbles his name and takes the bag. "Anything else?"

"Nope, you're free to go."

"Come on, let's wait outside," his dad says. "The smells in here!"

His dad goes first, holding the heavy door open for him and he steps through into the bright afternoon, blinking furiously as his eyes adjust to the light.

"I could do with a beer," Noah groans as his dad comes to stand next to him, hands in his pocket.

"Yeah, and a cigarette."

"I suppose both are out of the question," Noah

mumbles.

"You know your mum."

He kicks at the ground and then halts, his dad stiffening beside him too, sensing the same thing. Cora.

He spots her dashing across the road, her hair flying behind her as she runs. She's wearing a plain, yellow dress that makes the colour of her eyes pop, and her cheeks are flushed pink. When she reaches their side of the road she keeps running, straight towards him.

He tries to make sense of it. Why is she here? Is she angry? Concerned? But he finds he doesn't care. Seeing her is like taking a long drink of water after a trek through the desert. He could happily stand and soak her in all day.

"Noah!" she says, flinging her arms around him and burying her face in his chest.

"Cora?" Cautiously, he wraps her in an embrace, unsure what this means.

Beside him, his dad arches an eyebrow, stepping aside.

"Why didn't you tell them where you were?" she says, her body shaking.

"I... I don't know. Because you told me not to, I guess."

"Fuck! I don't want you to end up in jail."

"Really?"

She squints up at him. Her eyelashes are wet.

"Of course not." she says. "Why the hell would you think that?" Her hands clasp at him. "I'm so sorry. I messed up."

She smells amazing — as always — the scent seeming to invade his pores and take over his senses. He knows no matter what this woman does to him, he'll never not forgive her. All this talk, all this bullshit, about Alphas and their dominance, their abuse of power, and it's this little Omega who has him under her control. And he doesn't care one bit. Holding her in his arms is the best feeling in the world. Assuming he'd never get to do it again had been misery.

"Did you tell them, Cora? Is that why they let me go?" She nods, one lone tear sliding down her cheek. He wipes it away with his thumb. "You didn't have to come down here for me."

"Don't be silly."

He wants to ask her if he's a fool to raise his expectations, but he can't find the words and neither can he let her go.

Behind him, his dad coughs.

He takes Cora's hand in his own and spins around.

"You're the young lady who has been occupying so much of my son's time," his dad says with a grin.

"This is Cora, Dad."

"Hi," Cora says.

"She confirmed to the police where I was at the time of the assault."

"And they believed you?" his dad asks.

"Cora can be pretty forceful." He squeezes her hand and she leans into his arm, stroking her thumb along his little finger. In his chest his heart thumps a little stronger, but he daren't hope.

"Well why don't we get some food, you kids must be starving and you can tell us all about it."

Noah shakes his head. "Cora wouldn't —"

"I'd love to," she interrupts.

"Great. I'll just see if I can drag your mum away from whatever it is she's doing in there." His dad waves towards the station.

"Probably threatening to sue them," Noah says.

"Ha! Probably!"

Noah waits for him to leave, then turns to Cora. He still has hold of her hand, he's not letting go.

"I missed you," she says.

He swallows away a lump in his throat. "I missed you too...a lot." He interlocks his fingers through hers. "In fact, it hurt."

She peers up into his eyes. "We seem to be good at hurting each other."

"No," he says, "I'm happy when we're together. It hurts when we're apart."

"I don't want us to be apart..." Her bright blue eyes lock on his. "I want to do this properly. No more secrets, or lies, or creeping about."

He puffs out a long stream of air. "I'd like that." Trailing a hand up her arm and over her shoulder, he cups the back of her head and bends down, resting his forehead against hers. "I'd like that."

She reaches up and strokes his cheek, and he closes his eyes against her soft touch. When he opens them again, she's gazing at him with something that looks like affection and he holds her closer, tilting his head to capture her lips in his. She tastes just the same as she always does, and it's familiar and grounding, her lips wet and warm. He caresses them gently between his, pressing her mouth into his with one hand, the other at the small of her back.

There's another loud cough behind them. He sighs into her mouth, then releases her and turns around.

His dad stands with his mum at his side. She's dressed in her office suit, peering at them both with curiosity.

"Mum, this is Cora," he hesitates, "my erm..."

"Girlfriend?" his mum asks.

"Yes," Cora says, holding out her hand for his mother to shake.

"Rosamund," his mother says, gripping Cora's hand in both of hers.

"Robert," says his dad, smiling and clapping his hands together. "Let's get that food then. How about that pub by the river? What was it called?"

"The White Elephant," Noah tells him.

"Yes, that's it," his dad says, clicking his fingers.

"Okay, can you give us a moment?" Noah says.

"Meet us by the car then," his mum says, dragging his dad away. "We're parked in that car park over the street."

"You sure about this?" he asks Cora, cradling her by the elbows and staring into her eyes.

"Yes, I am. Are you?"

"I've wanted to be with you forever." He smiles at her shyly.

"You have?"

He chuckles. "Yes, I have. I caught your scent that very first day at uni and you've been driving me mad ever since."

"Oh." She sweeps his hair behind his ear. "You never said."

"I'm trying to be a better person, Cora."

"Me too," she says.

"You've always been good — too good for me."

"No, I haven't. You were right. What you said that first time. What is the use of all that stuff I was doing when I couldn't even treat you right? The person I care about." He goes to interrupt her, but she shakes her head, placing her finger on his lips. "And Noah, you are a good person. You need to start believing it."

He smiles at her, attempting to snatch her finger between his lips. "Can I kiss you again, now, please?"

"You're asking? You never usually ask permission." She raises an eyebrow.

"Maybe there are things people agree to in a relationship. You know, what they like and don't like. We could do that."

"Yes, we could."

"So can I kiss you again?"

She stands on her tiptoes and kisses him passionately, whipping his breath away, and he feels giddy with it. Giddy and happy.

◆ ◆ ◆

Rose is in the kitchen when they return to her place later that evening. Cora takes a deep breath and leads him in.

"Is she going to yell at me?" he whispers into her ear, his fingertips on her hip bone.

"We need to thank her," she whispers back. They walk inside and she points to a chair, grinning when he looks up nervously at her. Well, Rose is the closest thing she has to family — it's the equivalent of meeting her parents.

"Rose," she says, and Rose twists around, unplugging her earphones.

"Cora!" She hugs her. "Are you okay? Did it go okay?"

"Yes, Dr Pearson was amazing; cut through all the bullshit. We were out of there in less than 20 minutes. And look who else is out." She gestures toward him with her thumb.

"Oh, hi Noah."

"Hi. Thank you for your help." Noah says, nodding at her.

"That's okay. We want the real attackers caught."

He bows his head. Then drags his hand over his face, meeting her eye "Do... do people really think I'm capable of doing something like that?" His body becomes suddenly heavy with sadness and Cora bites her lip.

Rose considers. "You don't have the best reputation and I guess that prejudices people against you, but I was genuinely shocked you'd attack a lone woman... that didn't seem like you."

He nods. "Thank you. Not exactly the greatest start to the last term."

"Yeah," Cora says, leaning against the counter and brushing back her hair. "And my revision hasn't gone well."

"Mine either," he says, and she meets his eyes. "I've had too much on my mind."

He feels the severity of her look and sees her cheeks warm.

"Ha! As if either of you need to revise!" Rose snorts. "You're both top of your class."

"I don't know," Cora muses.

Rose takes a seat at the table. "What're your plans after graduation, Noah?"

Cora's eyes flit to him. They've never talked about the future before. He has no idea what she will do or where she will go. A tiny sense of panic swims through his veins. It must be noticeable, but she pretends not to register it.

"I've got a place at Saracens rugby club summer training academy." He glances sideways at Cora. "I'm hoping if I can impress them, I might get a contract."

"Really? Wow."

"I mean, who knows," he adds. "It's extremely competitive, but I'd prefer it to an office job, even if the money won't be great."

"I thought sportsmen earned loads."

"Only the stars."

Rose waves her hand at him. "Not that you need the money."

Noah smiles sheepishly.

It's the other thing they've never spoken about. She must know he's wealthy, but perhaps she hadn't appreciated how wealthy until that meal with his parents. He caught the way she stared at his dad's watch, worth enough to probably wipe away all her debts, and the manner in which her mouth had gaped wider and wider as they'd talked about their house in London, ski trips to their lodge in the Alps, and vacations to their home in the Caribbean. He has never flaunted it. But now she must realise he has far more money than he'd let on. She stares at her feet.

"How about you, Cora? What are you going to do?" He gazes at her, trying to keep his face neutral.

"I'd like to work for a lobbying group like Organised Omegas of the World or Future Mates, but it's competitive and I couldn't afford to intern."

Six months ago he would have laughed at that and derided her. Now he frowns with thought.

"You'd be great at that. It sucks," Rose says.

"I could talk to my mum," Noah says. "She has loads, and I mean loads, of links to those organisations. I'm sure she could get you a position."

"Isn't that nepotism or something?"

"Fuck that!" Rose says.

Noah chuckles. "Trust me, my mum would only pull her strings if she thought you were good enough."

"But I couldn't afford it. London is so expensive."

He pauses, reflecting. "Yeah, it is."

She peers at him, the silence awkward.

"I'm going to go and revise," Rose says. "I'm glad things worked out for you guys." She smiles at Cora with big 'oh my gosh' eyes and leaves them to it.

She creeps towards him, peering down at him with those sky-blue eyes.

"We're really doing this then, Cora? You and me? Officially? I mean, I can tell people you're mine?" He's talking very quickly as he pulls her towards him and she climbs into his lap. He fixes her gaze with his.

She nods, burying her fingers in his hair.

A wide smile spreads across his face. "Fuck," he murmurs.

They try to be quiet for Rose's sake, but it's been an age since he slipped inside her, filling her up and holding her firm. Despite the urgency, the pace is slow and languid. He takes the time to kiss every part of her from the tips of her toes, to the glands on the insides of her wrists, until he's certain her skin is alive and tingling and she's begging for release.

When he's satisfied her with his tongue and his fingers, he lifts her up into his lap and she wraps her legs around him. They hold each other closely, losing themselves in each other's eyes as she rocks and grinds onto him, driving him wild with the achingly slow pace, allowing their orgasms to build and build and build, and he loses all reason and all constraint, focused only on how perfect she feels and how much he wants her.

CHAPTER
TWENTY ONE

"Time's up. Please put down your pens."

Cora folds the papers closed and glances around at the other students, all doing the same. She shifts in her seat and catches Noah's eyes as he looks up from his own exam papers. He smiles and she grins, twisting back around in her chair and sinking down, allowing relief to sweep through her.

Over. Finally, it's all over. University officials dressed in their long black capes sweep along the rows collecting up the papers and then one-by-one dismiss each of the students.

She fiddles with the red carnation pinned to her own much shorter gown until her line is given the nod to go. She hovers in the hallway waiting for Noah, and he gives her another big grin as he hurries to reach her, grasping her hand.

"How did it go?" she whispers.

"Okay, I think," he says. "You?"

"Yeah, good."

He grips her hand and they step out of the dark corridor and into the bright June afternoon, the light hitting their eyes. She blinks.

"Cora! Cora!"

She swings her gaze about until she spots Rose and Zach waiting for her in the crowd.

"Go on," Noah tells her, and suddenly he's yanked away from her and swamped by his rugby team mates.

She pushes her way through the groups of students to her friends, a cloud of glitter exploding over her head as she nears them, coating her in sparkles. Rose wraps her in a hug, squeezing her tight, then shoves her away. Cora stumbles and before she catches her bearing, Zach pops the cork from a bottle of champagne and, shaking it vigorously, fires foam at her.

"Hey," she squeals, shielding her eyes with her hands.

"Congratulations," Zach yells, handing her the bottle.

She takes a swig and throws back her head.

"Woohoo!" she screams.

Rose ties a golden star helium balloon to the hood of her gown and empties another canon of confetti over her. Then she crushes her in a second hug.

"Come on," Zach says, "let's go celebrate."

"One moment," Cora elbows her way to Noah.

He's tangled in silly string and someone has sprayed his hair red. "Noah," she yells, shaking up the champagne bottle. He turns around and she shoots him with the alcohol, giggling as she does.

"Hey!" He opens his arms and dashes towards her. She swerves to the side, and aims more foam at his face. He lunges, catching her, wrapping her in a bear hug, nustling his mouth in her neck, and tickling his way down her sides until she's laughing so violently she can't catch her breath. "Let's go to the pub," he says, snatching the bottle and taking a long gulp.

She waves Zach and Rose over and they follow Noah and his friends across the main Oxford road, past the Bodleian Library and down the side streets, ducking into one of the alleyways to sit in the courtyard of an old Oxford pub.

They order more champagne and several plates of chips and cram around a picnic table.

Rose threads her arm through Cora's. "I have something to show you," she whispers into her ear as the others talk around them.

"What?"

Rose tugs her phone from her pocket and activates the screen. It lights up and she slips it to Cora. Taking the phone in her palm and angling it towards her, Cora frowns quizzically at Rose and then peers down at the display.

It's a photo of a newborn baby, all chubby and pink, its face screwed shut and a woollen hat pulled over the crown of its head.

"It's my sister," Rose says, gazing over Cora's shoulder. "Vera-Mae. She was born this morning."

"She's adorable Rose," Cora coos, taking her friend's hand in hers. "Are you okay, though?"

"Yeah, she's too gorgeous not to be, and it isn't her fault that she has such shitty parents."

"She's going to need a decent big sister like you to look out for her." Cora squeezes her hand and passes back the phone.

Rose stares at the picture of the baby. "I think we'll have lots of fun together."

"Totally."

"Move up girls," Zach says, two bottles of beer balanced in either hand as he slides onto the bench between them.

More of their friends arrive and others leave. The afternoon sun starts to dip and soon it's dark. The pub's courtyard heaves, people crowding around the picnic tables, leaning against walls, or sitting on patches of grass.

Cora's hair is sticky with champagne and glitter, and her carnation wilts on her chest. Noah has gone to talk to a group of economics students on another table, but he glances over to her now and jerks his head.

She nods.

"I'm going to go," she whispers into Rose's ear, kissing her cheek.

"Really?" Rose moans, resting her head on Cora's shoulder, her eyes squiffy from the drinks. "The night's still young!!"

"I'll catch you later," she says, clambering to her feet, her skin already dancing from the feel of Noah's gaze.

As she approaches, he slinks his arm around her shoulder. His hands are so big they could engulf her waist and she realises in that moment how much she likes being held by her Alpha. Despite all those things she'd heard and known about him, there was always this primal sensation of safety in his arms.

The streets are full of students, some singing and some dancing, plus little groups of tourists snapping photos and watching the celebrations. The tourists stare at Cora and Noah, dressed in their gowns, as they pass them, strolling away from the centre of town and out towards Magdalen.

As they near the bridge, Noah unhooks his arm and takes her elbow, pulling her down towards the river.

"Come on," he says, "let's go out on the water."

"It's pitch black," she protests, letting him draw her along. "And all the boats will be locked up for the evening."

"Nah." They reach the edge of the water. Rows of punts are lined up under the bridge stretching from one bank to the other. He peers across the dark surface. "There's always one or two that don't get locked up."

"How do you know that?" she says, eyeing him

suspiciously.

He grins. "Ha! There's one." He jumps down onto the nearest punt and clambers across the path of boats until he reaches the one he's spotted. "Come on!"

She climbs into the first, the balloon Rose had given her bumping against her crown, and carefully makes her way across to him. "Are we going to get arrested for this?"

"No." He gestures for her to take a seat and standing at the rear of the punt, pulls the pole from under the seats and pushes them away. His action is forceful and they zoom across the river straight towards the bank. He yanks down on the stick, bringing the boat to a sudden halt, then he changes the angle and drives off again, this time hurtling towards the other bank.

Cora shakes her head. "Why can nobody else punt?! Let me do it?" She holds out her hand to him and he throws her an unamused look. "You're not going to pull some Alpha bullshit, are you?" she says, standing with her hand on her hip.

"No Ma'am," he hands her the pole and, adjusting the seats, lies back in the boat, arms behind his head, and gazes up at her. "I'm not going to complain when I get to enjoy a view like this."

"I'm hardly looking my best." She gazes down at her dark skirt, white blouse, and black gown.

"You always look incredible." He winks at her.

They're silent while she glides the punt along, squinting through the night to follow the curvature of the river, and emerging through the trees, away from the city and out into the meadow. The night is clear and the sky scattered with bright stars, reflected like fireflies on the water.

"Come here," he says, his voice thick, and she tucks away the pole, kneeling down into the belly of the boat. He stops her with his hand, reaching behind her to untie the balloon from her gown, and they watch together as he lets it go and it floats up into the twinkling heavens. Then she lies down beside him, her head resting on his arm.

"I can't believe university is over," she says, his scent heavy in her nose.

"Yeah." The tips of his fingers caress along her sides. She can tell he's thinking like she is, about the past, about the future, about now. "When's your interview for the internship?"

"Next week, but I'm not sure there's any point in going. I can't afford to live in London without a wage."

"I've been thinking, you could come and live with me."

She twists her head, searching for his face in the twilight. "Live with you?"

"I mean, not forever or whatever. Just until you get a paid position or find your own place." His whole body is tense beside hers.

"Are you serious?" It's fast, very fast and maybe it isn't the right, or sensible, thing to do but the thought of waking up to him every day has her heart skipping.

"Yes. I am. My parents have a flat in their basement that's mine. It's self-contained and big enough for two. I don't pay rent." He rolls her towards him. "But you wouldn't have to live in the flat with me, you could stay in the guest room. It probably sounds crazy—"

"It is crazy."

"It's not marriage or mating. If it doesn't work out, it doesn't work out."

She rests her hand on the centre of his chest. "I want to live with you, Noah."

"Is that a yes then?"

"Yes, it's a yes. A cautious yes, a 'let's see how things go' yes."

"You know I love you," he whispers and she does, feels it deep inside her with no doubt and no question.

"Hmmm. Is that what this fuzzy, warm feeling is?" she murmurs, the almost-full moon gazing down on her. She finds his hand, threading her fingers through his. "Then I think I must love you too, Noah."

His scent spirals around her, content and blissful, and she smells the way hers mixes with it, complementing it, as if their aromas were somehow always meant to belong together, entwined in this way.

The boat rocks gently and she stares up at the vast open sky, free at last.

Yes, this is what it is to be loved.

EPILOGUE

Two years later

The stadium rumbles with the hoards of fans chanting and singing, the structure vibrating beneath her feet as Cora squeezes along the row, Zach and Rose trailing behind her. She spots Noah's dad waving at her, and weaves her way towards him.

"It's so big," Zach yells over the noise. "I had no idea the stadium would be this big, or this noisy." He grimaces and Cora smiles, taking his hand and leading them to their seats. They are bigger and more comfortable than the fold-up ones the majority of fans have, but nobody is sitting.

Robert greets her with a peck on the cheek and the squeeze of her shoulders, then shakes hands with the others. He has a huge grin plastered across his face like an excited schoolboy.

"Full stadium," he says, jerking his thumb above them. She turns her head and looks up, instantly dizzy from the thousands and thousands of rows of faces, and she snaps back around, snuggling into her thick coat and burying her nose in Noah's scarf. She'd pinched it this morning, knowing his scent would calm her later. She inhales it now, closing her eyes as the clock counts down and stirring music blasts out over the speakers.

"You will explain the rules, won't you?" Rose says, leaning across Zach to get to Cora.

"It's just like American football," Zach tells her.

Cora shakes her head. "It's not," she says, but her voice comes out in a squeak.

"You okay, Cora?" Noah's dad asks, leaning into her.

"Yes," she says. "I just wish they'd start already — this build-up is driving me mad."

Robert nods his head as a roar erupts around the crowd. "Here they come now."

She scans quickly along the line of players snaking out onto the grass. There he is, in his freshly pressed kit, one of the tallest of the squad, his long hair scraped back in a bun. He looks neither nervous or excited but focused, and she knows in that moment it will be a good game for him. He's been on the bench the whole season, making the odd sub appearance, but this is his first start and they'd jumped around the kitchenette together when the manager had called to tell him.

Living together has been full of little moments like that — ones she wants to file away in her mind. Memories she knows she wants to keep and relive. A mixture of shared leaps around the kitchen — when she was offered a permanent position at Organised Omegas of the World, when they got the keys to their own flat — and the everyday routine of being together.

They make a good team. They both know it, and so does everyone else. He is her support, she is his comfort. They make each other happy.

"There he is!" says Rose, pointing towards him, and bouncing up and down on the spot. "Quick, get a photo Zach."

Down on the grass, she sees Noah scan the box where the players' families sit until he spots her and catches her eye. Then it's as if every other person in the stadium melts away. It's just the two of them; he could almost be stood right there in front of her.

Good luck, sweetheart, she mouths. *Go get them.*

He places his hand over his heart.

I love you, he says, and she smiles. He smiles back, his eyes alight, hesitates, then fixes her eyes. *Marry me?*

Her face breaks with emotion, her whole body flooding with it, and she nods.

THE END

Want to read Noah and Cora's
extended epilogue?

Visit Hannah's website www.hannahhaze.com

To get your hands on another Hannah
Haze book for free, and to be the first to hear

about other goodies, sign up to Hannah's newletter on Hannah's website.

Did you enjoy this book? Please leave a review or rating.

Read on for an exclusive preview of Hannah's next book:

The Alpha Escort Agency

THE ALPHA ESCORT AGENCY

Chapter One

"Fuck it," Alice mutters, slamming the front door behind the quickly retreating back of the Alpha and closing her eyes in relief. Thank god he's gone. She stands there thinking for a moment, then rushes to the kitchen, flips open her laptop, and fires it up.

She needs to take a shower, really badly, change the sheets and clear up all this mess in the kitchen. I mean, what the hell has that dude done in here. It looks like he pulled open every cupboard door and helped himself to just about everything inside — including the very expensive chocolates her boss gave her for Christmas, which she'd been saving. He'd obviously been busy stuffing his face while she slept between their... yes, well... and yet he'd not once bothered to bring her a snack. In fact, she's bloody starving. She dashes to the cupboard and drags out the biscuit tin, cradling it onto her lap while the computer stirs into life and chomping on one, then a second and a third custard cream.

The clearing up can wait, she thinks, as she brushes biscuit crumbs off her chest and onto the floor. First, she is sorting this out once and for all, because there is no way, no way in hell, she is ending up stuck in heat with yet another deadbeat, arsehole Alpa. No way! And nor is she going to endure it alone with only a pathetically inadequate Alpha dildo to see her through the gut-searing cramps that always hit an Omega in heat without a good dose of Alpha cock.

No, next time she is going to be prepared and ready with a decent Alpha lined up, who will take care of her needs and, if what she's heard is true, her laundry too.

Alice types in her password and opens the web browser. She can't remember the name of the company — she'd only been half listening to the conversation at lunch that day when her boss, a fellow Omega, had whispered to them about how she'd hired an Alpha escort to help her through her heat. Maria had been full of questions, but Alice had dismissed it all. Yes, she'd heard of such services before, but really who needed to pay for such things when there was always a queue of Alphas more than happy to help an Omega in heat. Escorts were only for desperate Omegas. Why waste her money?

Except her boss, Lisa, is anything but

desperate. Beautiful, successful and sassy, she is the type of woman in charge of her life and choices. The type of woman that makes people fall desperately in love with her.

The type of woman Alice is now determined to be.

No more last-minute dashes to a bar to pick up some random Alpha at the start of a heat, no more hurried scrolling through the Alpha/Omega heat matching app at three in the morning when she can't take it anymore. Nope, those things only land her locked in bed with some guy who stinks of liquor, or has the IQ of a banana, or can't tell the difference between a clitoris and an anus.

Occasionally it's been even worse than that. There had been one guy who'd been a little too rough for her liking despite her protestations, and another who'd cleared out her emergency stash of cash.

Google throws up a surprising number of Alpha Omega Escort agencies, although the majority, surprise, surprise, are for men seeking women or other men. There are only a handful for women. She scrolls down, chugging back a bottle of water at the same time, still thirsty from her heat. The Alpha hadn't gone once to fetch her something to drink, despite that being one of the necessities for an Omega in heat. The increased body temperature and vigorous, erm, sex means it's easy for an Omega to become dangerously dehydrated.

When she replaces her glass and focuses back on the screen, she spots a name she thinks she recognises: The Alpha Escort Agency. Taking a deep breath in, she clicks on the link. The website is sleek and beautiful looking, with her marketing eye she can see it's been designed to appeal to a female clientele and is an expensive job. Somehow that reassures her — this isn't some fly by night, two bit outfit.

To her surprise, there are no photos of the Alpha escorts on the front page. It's like the classy sex shops she's been to in Soho: inviting but discrete. Although she wonders if the Alphas aren't pretty enough to put on the landing page. They are almost always hot - taller and more muscular than your average Beta and Omega, but sometimes Alice has to admit that they can look a little harsh, intimidating even.

Her brain spirals away down a rabbit hole. What kind of Alpha would want to be an escort? Sure, Alphas outnumber Omegas these days, which means there's lots of single Alphas out there. Some have resorted to hooking up with other Alphas or Betas. But she's pretty sure most Alphas have no problem with getting laid, so they wouldn't be doing this job for the sex. No, these men must do it for the money. They must be strapped for cash. Although working for a classy agency, rather than hanging about street corners or working in a brothel, must mean they earn decent wages.

The first doubts crawl in. These men must be creeps, right? There has to be something wrong with them?

She shakes her head. No! Lisa, much to her unease, had gushed about what a gentleman the Alpha who had seen to her had been. Handsome, well educated, good manners and an excellent cook.

She scans over the homepage text. There are promises of a discrete service, personalised to the needs of each individual client and differing packages with a range of prices.

'Here at the Alpha Escort Agency, we understand the sensitive and intimate situation a heat can present. You want security, comfort and companionship. Whether you're looking for a regular companion to see you through your monthly heat or are in search of one off help, all our experienced Alpha escorts are trained to ensure you are well cared for. All personal preferences and desires catered for. Our escorts will even launder your bedding and cook your dinner.'

Alice peers around at her trashed kitchen and thinks that sounds like a winning idea.

She clicks through onto the different packages. Now there are pictures of the Alphas. All soft focus, nicely lit. They are dressed in fluffy boyfriend sweaters, smiling and laughing, or peering into the camera with a wistful longing that gives her butterflies in her stomach. The photographs are certainly a contrast to the ones the alphas usually post on their profiles — all topless, strained muscles and fierce faces — sometimes even a dick pic. Yuck! This agency has a much better idea of what women want — well, women like her anyway.

The premium, platinum, all singing, all dancing package doesn't even have a price listed, so she's pretty sure that is out of her budget. The next one down is pretty bank breaking. But after that it's not so bad. After all, she's a single woman with a good job, fast approaching her thirties who owns her own apartment, has company gym membership, no pets, no kids and no hobbies. In other words, she has plenty of disposable income. What is she going to spend it on if not this? Another singles holiday to a yoga retreat in Bali where she'll end up with a sore back and a bad case of the runs?

Yes, this is a much better investment. She pulls up the application form and fills it out. For a moment she considers using a false name, but, what the hell, she has nothing to be ashamed of. There's quite a bit of small print, but again she finds that reassuring. It's stuff about the need to vet clients in advance, including testing for STDs, and for clients and escorts to use protection. No communicating with the employees is permitted outside the arrangement, no recording equipment allowed during the shared heats and no requests for photographs of genitalia. Heats are to be shared at the client's home or one of the pre-approved hotels. Certain acts are banned, but she isn't even sure what half of those are. Finally, there's a promise to be in touch within twenty-four hours.

Alice hits send and heads for the shower, feeling pleased she's finally taking control of this mess that is her sex life.

On Monday morning, Maria slides into her office between meetings and drags her out to get a coffee. Maria used to be the person Alice went out drinking and dancing with on a weekend but Maria has been happily cocooned in a relationship for the last eighteen months and now she lives vicariously through Alice, although Alice seems to spend more and more time working late or home alone.

"So?" Maria asks, bumping her shoulder into Alice's as they stand in queue.

"So what?" Alice says, suddenly keen to search her handbag for her purse.

"Oh, no! No no no!" Maria wags her finger at Alice wildly. "Don't give me that — details now please or I won't be your back up next time."

Maria and Alice used to have an arrangement. When either was in heat, they'd send details of the Alpha they were spending it with. It was a safety net, just in case things went wrong. However, Alice is the only one that's been making use of this arrangement since Maria hooked up with Ed and unfortunately that means she's the only one supplying all the gory details of hopeless Alphas and forgettable heats.

"I don't want to talk about it," says Alice with a mixture of a blush and a frown.

"That bad, huh?"

"Worse."

The tall man in front of them steps aside and they reach the counter.

"Hello ladies, what will it be?" asks the enthusiastic barista.

"Two frappuccinos." Maria glances at Alice and squeezes her arm. "And you'd better add extra cream and chocolate syrup in hers."

"Bad day?" the server asks sympathetically.

"Something like that," Alice grimaces, pinning a stray lock of her black curled hair back into her French plait.

When they're seated on one of the low walls in the courtyard between the tall tower blocks, Maria restarts her inquisition.

"Was it the sex?" she says, peering across the rim of her paper cup.

Alice dips her finger into the whipped cream, scooping some onto her finger and then sucking it into her mouth.

"No," she licks her lips, "just the usual jerk. Ate me out of house and home, yet failed to feed me once or even bring me a goddamn glass of water. I had to keep dragging myself to the bathroom."

"Bloody hell!" Maria shakes her head, her shiny red hair cut about her chin, shimmering as she does. "Who raised these Alphas? Why do none of them seem to know the first thing about heat etiquette? It's not that hard — especially considering what they're getting in return."

"I'm thinking of giving up on them altogether," Alice says, scooping up more cream.

"What, Alphas?" Maria stares at her, shock written across her face. "But going through a heat alone would be..." she shivers, "hell."

"Oh God, no!" Alice's brow crinkles with deep lines. "I mean random Alphas. No more hookups. I've signed up to the Alpha Escort Agency."

Maria nearly drops her coffee. "What?!"

"I looked it up and it actually seems the perfect solution for me." Maria examines her face, her mouth still hanging open. Alice turns her head to glance at her. "What?" She reaches out and shakes her friend. "Maria!"

"Well...I mean..."

"It worked for Lisa."

"Lisa is not a romantic."

"Neither am I."

Maria snorts. "Oh, yes you are. You just pretend not to be. I know you, Alice Turner." She reaches out and pinches Alice on the arm.

"Ow!" Rubbing her arm, she scowls at her friend. Her best friend, actually. They have been since they hit it off on Alice's first day of work, Maria assigned to show her round and kindly filling her in on all the office gossip.

"At all costs stay out of the path of Mrs Clackeridge." she'd advised wisely.

"Mrs?"

"Oh yeah. I don't even know what her first name is but she hates all of us young ones. Especially if you touch her precious stationery supplies without asking."

"Okay."

"And that's Pete. He seems friendly and sweet and will probably offer to help at some point over the next few days, but he's a mega creepy slime ball. Just tell him to go away. Oh, and that's Janet who is having an affair with Tanya. It's been going on for like a year and everybody knows about it but for some reason they insist on keeping it secret." Maria had shrugged after that, hooked her arm through Alice's and dragged her to lunch.

Now Maria rolls her brown eyes at Alice. "I don't know why you don't try dating like everyone else."

"Because you know I'm not interested in finding anyone right now, Maria. The life plan."

"I know, the life plan," Maria mutters.

Alice ignores her and holds up her fingers. "Step one: Get marketing degree — tick. Step two: Secure position in one of the top three marketing agencies — tick. Step three: purchase own property — tick. Step four: land promotion and become an account director — yet to be accomplished. All this by the time I'm thirty and then I might think about dating." She wants her own life, her own security. She doesn't want to build her entire existence around another person, not like her mum had, because when that person is gone she'd have nothing left.

Maria rolls her eyes again. "Where's the fun in it, though? The spontaneity?"

"We aren't all lucky enough to have a flourishing career and find Mr Perfect, you know. So some of us have to take matters into our own hands and find other arrangements."

"Hmmm." Maria shifts on the wall and looks out towards the fountain.

"What?" Alice examines her. "What's up?"

"I don't know. Maybe Ed isn't Mr Perfect after all."

"What?" A slosh of coffee lands by Alice's feet as she flings her arms into the air. "He is."

"I don't know; things have felt a bit off lately."

Alice waits, but Maria says nothing more and she knows not to push her friend. She'll tell her when she's good and ready. Trying to force things out of Maria only results in her clamming up.

Alice sips her coffee. "So anyway. They've already matched me to a suitable escort."

This tugs Maria out of her reverie. "They

have?"

"Yes. They've offered an introductory meeting before my actual heat to check I'm happy. Do you think I should meet him or just wait for my heat?"

"No, meet him. Definitely meet him. You don't want another twot."

◆ ◆ ◆

The Alpha Escort Agency available on Amazon and Kindle Unlimited.

HANNAH HAZE
BOOKS

ONLINE HEAT - available on Amazon

Trapped on her own during lockdown, Maya begins to fall for her boss and director of the company, Max Harrison. Tall, broad and strong with strikingly blue eyes; all her Omega senses tell her he must be an Alpha. Their meetings may be virtual but they are the most real thing in Maya's life right now and she suspects he may feel the same way too.

But when her heat strikes, the stakes between them rise and their reckless and passionate actions endanger both their professional careers and their hearts.

THE ALPHA ESCORT AGENCY - available on Amazon

Alice Turner is hiring an Alpha Escort.

No more random hook-ups. No more lousy Alphas. She's paying for a man to see her through her heat, and clean her dishes and wash her sheets too. It's the perfect arrangement for an Omega like her, one who's not interested in romance.

Rory's one successful escort. Dedicated to each assignment, guaranteed to deliver satisfaction and ruggedly good-looking. It's the perfect job for an Alpha like him. He can satisfy certain urges, pay the rent and subsidise his hobby. All while keeping his heart well protected. Because agency rules dictate: no relationships with clients.

And he can't risk his livelihood for some little Omega; no matter how delicious she may smell, and no matter how cute she may be.

CHRISTMAS HEAT - available on Amazon

What smells better than Christmas?

The mystery Omega.

Joe smells her everywhere.

Now he can finally track her down.

But will meeting the woman whose mesmerising scent has been driving him wild turn out to be the perfect Christmas miracle? Or a nightmare before Christmas?

ABOUT THE AUTHOR

Hannah Haze

Hannah writes soft and steamy romances, sure to get your pulse racing and your heart fluttering. Her couples are destined to find each other - and when they do, oh boy!

Hannah Haze loves long romantic walks in the countryside, undisturbed soaks in a hot bath and even hotter stories.

Hannah lives close enough to London to take advantage of city delights, but far enough away to explore muddy woods and fields with her husband and children.

To find out more, visit Hannah's website www.hannahhaze.com

ACKNOWLEDGE-MENT

Thank you to my beta readers Hannah and Lydia for all their help and to Mr D for his ongoing love, support and very sexy spreadsheets.

Printed in Great Britain
by Amazon

33507117R00139